"Now that's what I call a right pretty sight," George stated quietly as he walked up behind Jake. The tall white man jumped as though someone had stuck him with a knife. "By gawd," he roared, "you got the nerve!" His eyes went to the pistol George held. "That's Jamie's pistol, boy. You really done somethin' to my young brother." George laughed in his face. "Naw, I ain't did nothing to him. Them 'gators back in the pond did it for me. Yes sir! Them 'gators had a damn good time with all that stinkin' white meat!"

Donald Goines

SWAMP MAN

HOLLOWAY HOUSE PUBLISHING CO.
LOS ANGELES, CALIFORNIA

Published by
HOLLOWAY HOUSE PUBLISHING COMPANY
8060 Melrose Avenue, Los Angeles, California 90046

International Standard Book Number 0-87067-191-X
Printed in the United States of America
Cover photography by Jeffrey. Posed by professional models.

Dedicated To
my mother, Myrtle Goines, who had confidence in
my writing ability.

DG

1

THE SUN HAD JUST COME UP when George Jackson pushed back some of the tall brown willow weeds he was hiding behind. He could now make out some of the wild ducks swimming in the creek. Even with the appearance of the sun over the tree tops it was still dark in the Mississippi swamp. George decided to wait until it became lighter before trying for one of the geese.

A tall husky boy of fourteen, George already had the build of a man. It was evident that he would be an exceptionally powerful man when he was full grown. Suddenly he grew tense. An alarm inside of him started to tick. It was his swamp sense and told him that danger was near. His huge shoulders became tense, a large vein in his neck began to swell. His eyes darted back and forth. Not a muscle moved. He could have passed for a wooden statue.

As George's huge hands inched toward the trigger on the shotgun, he saw the danger approaching out of the corner of his eye. The deadly water moccasin was already three feet out of the water and halfway up the narrow bank.

The large poisonous snake had become intrigued with the warm-blooded creature it smelled. And as George watched, the snake started to slither toward him. He couldn't help but admire the way the reptile seemed to glide over the broken surface of the slimy ground.

George would have been in trouble if he hadn't been a swamp man. Before his father's death, the man had taken his son deep into the swamps, revealing byways to the young boy that were known by only a handful of men.

Suddenly the snake changed its course and went around him. George watched it enter the water, then go under. He smiled to himself as he realized what was happening. The snake was lying in ambush. If George should step anywhere near where the snake had hidden, he would be taking a chance on getting bitten. His eyes drifted over to the small dugout, checking to make sure none of the moccasin's brothers had taken an interest in his homemade canoe. But there was only the thin paddle and a stick eight feet long, important to the survival of any man who frequented the dangerous back waters.

It was now light enough to shoot. George raised the shotgun to his shoulder. He could see four ducks swimming together. Then he pulled the trigger. The gunshot rang out in the stillness of the morning. He rushed over to his dugout, his boots making a swishy sound as he ran through the slime. He moved now by instinct, pushing out into the water, keeping his eyes on the two birds that he knew he had killed.

Before the sound of the gunshot had died, the other birds had taken to the wing. One could hear the rustle from the trees as other animals and birds took flight. The gunshot warned them that their most dangerous enemy was near.

George had one problem now confronting him. If he didn't reach his birds in time, one of the other carnivorous beasts of prey might beat him to his meal. He didn't have to worry about the alligators. They had been hunted too much by man. They were cautious now, laying on their mounds of earth and sunning themselves. Then, at the first warning of the approach of man, they would slide into the murky water and disappear. George thought about the alligators as he reached out and pulled in his first bird. With his long pole, he pulled the other one closer, then reached out and scooped it out of the water.

George remembered how it used to be when his father had first started bringing him into the swamps. 'Gators used to be everywhere. Now, you had to hunt them down. It wasn't a hard task for a person like George, but 'gator hunting was a job he didn't like. He could stand snakes, but alligators he disliked. It was the way they dragged their victims underneath the water and buried them, waiting until the corpse became rotten. That was the way they liked their meat—stinking to high heaven. The thought of such a death filled him with dread.

George shook his head, trying to shake off the bad thoughts. This should be a day of happiness. His older sister would be coming home from college today. She had written last week and said she would come home for a visit. It would be the first time in two years, ever since she had received her scholarship from Lincoln College. It had taken some doing, or so she had said, but she had finally gotten one. It was a way to get out of the swamps—away from the white trash she had always despised. Even before the murder of their father, she had hated the southern whites, never speaking to them when they passed on the road.

George used his eight foot pole to push the small dugout along faster. He passed the first cotton patch, which meant that he was getting out of the swamp. The cotton stalks were bent and broken. The small patch obviously wasn't being cared for. George knew why that was. This was an old cotton patch, and it had been worked by blacks. The little field was too deep into the swamps for the whites to really care about it. His grandfather used to tend the place, but he was too old now, and George, next to hating alligators, hated cotton so the field went untended. The white trash, using the cotton as their bridge to the past, acted like old slave masters and got away with it.

There was a small corn field up ahead and George poled his boat toward it. He dragged it up to dry land and left it under a thicket of sycamore trees. It was quiet and clean under the tall trees, with just a small breeze shaking the limbs at the top.

George went into the field and picked the ripest ears of corn he could find, taking enough to last a few days. He carried them back and placed them in the dugout, again checking for snakes before putting his burden down. It was more from habit than anything else, but it was a good habit. Too many swamp people had died needlessly from the bite of a cottonmouth because they hadn't used their eyes. It was a habit his father had drilled into him—to always look—because in the swamps death could be waiting around the next bend.

As George pushed his small boat back into the water, the only sounds he could hear were those of the swamp. Frogs, crickets, an old owl in a tree somewhere. The noise was like a soothing massage. George gave one vigorous push with the long pole and the boat cut swiftly through the water.

The closer he got to home, the less caution he used. Just the thought of seeing his sister Henrietta again made his chest swell. He tried to remember how she looked the last time he had seen her. They were standing at the bus stop, waiting for the Greyhound bus. He had walked the five miles to town, carrying her two little suitcases. She could have managed without his aid, but he had wanted to go with her. There was a bond between them—a tie so deep that while she was away at college, she wrote twice a month, two letters at the same time, so that he wouldn't have to make a trip into town for nothing. She knew the way the mail was held at the small post office, so she wrote him according to that schedule. Every other Friday he would go into town, and sure enough there would be a letter for him. Sometimes she even mailed a few dollars so he could buy the stamps to answer her letters. Sometimes, she sent small lessons for him to do, even though she knew he went to the small school on Master Wilson's plantation. She was always trying to teach him things herself.

"Boy," he said to himself, "you goin' bust your big mouth wide open if you keep on grinnin'." He had spoken the words out loud and before he had finished talking he knew he had made a mistake. Somebody was coming around the bend on his left. It could only be the Jones boys, he realized quickly, and if there were any hillbillies he hated to come in contact with, it was the Jones boys—four brothers who lived on the high land, land that was swamp land, but dry enough to raise certain crops.

It was identical to what George's family did—raised crops to live on at the edge of the swamps. Only a few people lived like this. To most farmers, it was a poor way to earn a living. But George's father and grandfather had always said it was better than sharecropping—farming the land on one of the plantations and living as a tenant.

This way, they were independent. If they didn't

want to work, they didn't have to. Nor did they have to answer to anyone for what they did on the land. With a few chickens and pigs, a man could exist, but rarely did he see any cash money.

George eyed the bend to the right, which would take him down the lane that led to his house. He didn't believe he could make it before the loud-mouthed Jones boys came around from the opposite side.

And then they appeared. There were only two of them in their faded gray dugout, and if ever men looked a certain part, they looked theirs. White trash was written all over them. If this had been in the time of slavery, they would have been patrollers, men that ran down runaway slaves. Or, if not that, then members of the Confederate Army. But slavery had been outlawed over a hundred years ago, and these days the Jones boys had to settle for just being avid members of the Ku Klux Klan.

Both men had long, stringy, dirty blond hair that hung down in their faces. They were always tossing their heads back so that they could get the hair out of their eyes. Both men had pale blue eyes, with eyebrows so light that from a distance it didn't seem as if they had any eyebrows at all. The only difference between the two brothers was age. The one sitting in the front of the boat was the

14

youngest, still too green to grow a dirty, ill-shaped beard like his older brother.

"Nigger," the youngest Jones boy called out when they saw George, "ain't you got 'nough sense in that burr head not to be goin' 'round here talkin' to yourself?"

"Yes suh, Massah Jones," George answered, drawing out the words in a practiced southern drawl. It made the whiteys happy to be called master, but they also wanted it said in the old southern drawl. If a young black man wanted to get along with them, he practiced this whenever he came in contact with them. If not, he could bring trouble down on his head, or on members of his family. And on occasions like this, caught out in the swamps, without any witnesses, only a fool who didn't want to live to see tomorrow would resort to the trick. The blacks joked amongst themselves about it, but the joke was on them. They joked to take away the shame that they felt whenever they had to resort to its use. But for George, it hurt worse than ever. He had watched these same white men kill his father, and now here he sat, grinning and calling them "massah."

George thought about his sister. He had intended to keep straight down the river, so he could pick her up if she came in today as she said she would. But now, with the Jones boys going in that direction, he didn't want to follow along too close to them. He decided to take the birds home first. Maybe Henrietta hadn't caught the bus she had planned on catching, George reasoned. But George knew deep down inside that his reasoning was based on fear—the very real and urgent fear he had of the men who had murdered his father.

"What you so happy for, boy?" the younger brother drawled. " 'Cause Miss Nigger due this mornin'?"

"Jamie, shut your mouth boy, if'n you don't want my foot stuck down it!" the older brother stated harshly, cutting him off.

"That coon knows his place, Zeke," Jamie answered weakly, falling quickly into silence.

As George swung his boat into the bend on the right, his heart skipped a beat. They couldn't know, he thought. But then he realized that they did know. Old man Williams, who ran the post office, had been reading his mail again. There was no mistake, the Jones boys knew that Henrietta was due home today. Maybe that was the reason why they were on their way to town, just to abuse her verbally. That was all they could do, George believed. In a town full of people what else could they possibly do to his sister. This was the sixties, not the turn of the century when honkies could get away with anything. Nowadays, they had to walk a pretty straight line. Of course, what they did in the back country without witnesses was something else. Black people made sure they didn't get caught alone in the back country. But for people like George, there was little choice. They lived in the wild back country, and their only source of protection was themselves.

George made the slanting right hand turn into the S-shaped bend. The creek was much narrower here. There were trees on each side with long hanging vines. The green foliage on the left contrasted beautifully with the yellow of the tall cornfields swaying in the breeze. The morning smell of fresh air, mingled with the sweet chatter of birds, added still another dimension to the beauty of the river. But the young boy poling home did not notice these things. Under other circumstances, he might have stopped, stood up in the boat and inhaled deeply, enjoying the richness of nature.

A heavy premonition was on him as he paddled out of the last bend in the river's S-shaped curve and he came within sight of his home. Actually, there were two cabins. The first one stood high above the water on heavy log stalks. The stilts were so massive it seemed impossible that men had actu-

17

ally raised them. But men had—and the home sitting on the river had been the first cabin built on the land. George's father and grandfather had then cleared the surrounding land of stick brush, making the land ready for the planting of crops. Each year they were able to harvest enough corn, wheat and vegetables to feed the family. With the addition of wild meat and fish, the Jacksons were able to survive off the land.

George tied his dugout near the ladder that led to the catwalk. He had to push one of the other three boats away. The heavy rowboat was used when they had gone 'gator hunting, but George had discontinued that when he became the only hunter in the family. It was tied securely to the rear of the cabin by heavy vines that were woven together to make a thick rope. The other two boats were lighter dugouts similar in construction to the one George was using. One was built to carry at least three people, and the other one was identical to the one George had just finished securing to the dock.

George went up the ladder quickly, carrying only his shotgun and the two dead birds. The crudely made catwalk swayed under his weight. He hurried toward the ladder that led to dry ground. He had no reason to linger at the old house, because it was now used as a storage shack for fishing gear. Its other function was that of an outhouse, using the running water under the cabin to carry away the body waste. And what the water didn't get, the large, blackish-gray catfish that lingered underneath the cabin did.

The ground at the bottom of the ladder was firm. George ran up the well used pathway, passing the few scattered trees on each side. The grass near the pathway was short, the weeds had been cleared out to prevent the snakes from hiding in the brush and striking out at those who used the pathway.

This distance to the new cabin on the high ground was a good two hundred yards. As George neared the cabin door, a tall, gaunt black man stepped out the door. The sunshine played tricks with the gray hair on the elderly man's head, trying to find a dark spot in the thinning gray curls. Eyeglasses sat on the edge of his nose, revealing eyes that were dark from sorrow, hurt, and regret. A lifetime of despair was written on the man's lean face. Three scars ran down the right side of his face, lashes from long ago, that now looked like wrinkles in the dark brown skin.

The old man stepped aside and let the young boy enter. Neither one spoke. From habit the boy set the gun down at the door, then walked across the room and lay the birds on the crude handmade table.

As he turned to leave, George stopped and stared at the old man. "I'm goin' be needin' that, Pa."

George's grandfather continued on toward the table, carrying the shotgun and a cleaning rag. "Old Jefferson," the old man began in a soft drawl, "he was workin' in them white folks' bar last night, when he hear them Jones trash talkin' 'bout our girl coming home." The old man, who only had a first name because his father refused to give his freeborn son a slave name, was known as Ben. As the years passed, people started calling him Old Ben.

As he talked, Ben broke the gun down and reached for a rod. He glanced up at the boy who was quietly listening to him.

"You better be going, boy," Ben said, using the only term he ever used when speaking to George. It was a curious trait of the old man's. He would never use the boy's first or last name.

"I'm thinkin' I might need the shotgun, Pa," George stated quietly as he stood in front of the old man with his head down. He didn't want to look into those eyes because the boy was ashamed of his grandfather. Ashamed of the way his grandfather cringed when the whites were around. The old man couldn't help himself. He just shook. But the old man didn't tremble from fear. Instead, he shook from an inner rage, a feeling of frustration because he knew he was helpless.

"Not if'n yo' goin' after your sister. You goin' need both hands to help her with her bags," Ben stated as he rammed the rod down the barrel. Both man and boy knew what was not being said, that with whites you could never tell. The old man knew one thing for certain though and that was that the boy stood a better chance without the gun. He could tell that the boy had the same wild streak that his father had had. He was too quiet, staring out from his eyes at them as if to say there will be a judgment day.

"If'n you goin', boy, you better be hurryin'. She goin' be needin' your help," Old Ben said, trying to make the boy go without the gun.

As George stared down at the old man, he fought back the urge to take the gun from him. It just wasn't in him to use violence against Pa. And he knew the old man would resist.

Without another word, George started toward the door. When he stepped outside, he started to run toward the dugout. The river would be the quickest way, landing at the big bend and walking the rest of the way. The youth pushed off and guided his dugout down the muddy waters of the Mississippi and toward his long-awaited reunion with his sister.

2

HENRIETTA WATCHED CLOSELY as the bus moved quickly through Buckwater, Mississippi. Population of the small town was two hundred, not counting the blacks. The few houses they passed, were actually shacks. It would have been more appropriate to have called it Shanty Town. The crudely made outhouses could be seen in the rear of each dwelling.

The sight of the town made Henrietta sick. How she despised the place. She thought of her talented brother, with his ability to pick things up by himself. She remembered sending him the book on advanced math, thinking he could never understand it without some kind of help. Yet, reading slowly, he had learned from the book. If there was only some way of taking him out when I left, she thought. But their grandfather presented a problem. If she could talk the old man into leaving, then it could work. Once back in Atlanta, Georgia, she could get an agency to help. Then her dream of getting little George out of that swamp would come true.

The very thought of the swamp resurrected her hatred for the place. Hate wasn't the word. Loathing was more like it. The swamp was a loathsome thing, like the creepy, crawly creatures that lived there. Henrietta shivered and stood up as the bus parked in front of the whitewalled drugstore.

In front of the drugstore was a homemade, gray colored bench. Every day it was filled with the various white men who had tramped in from the farms and shanties. The drugstore also served as the hardware store, and was only one of two places you could buy your supplies. Next to it was the log cabin post office and the jail house. The street ended with the only bar and the other general store. That section was always busy at night when the two town whores were there.

Henrietta stepped from the bus with her two suitcases and looked around for George. She had just known that he would be there. Something must have happened, but what? She walked slowly past the staring men and stopped at the edge of the wooden walk. The rest of the way was a dirt road, leading toward the trail out of town. If George was coming, that was the way he would come.

As Henrietta watched for George, she noticed old man Jefferson waving at her. She figured she could get the old man to help her with the two suitcases she had brought with her. She gathered up her luggage and ran across the street to where Jefferson stood. She didn't notice the frowns on the white men's faces, but Jefferson saw it and read a warning in it.

As she came hurrying over, the old man said quickly, "Gal, get back on the bus! Hurry, if'n yo' don't wanna hav' troubl' out of them there crackers, 'cause they been sittin' and waitin' for yo' all mornin'."

"Why, that's impossible. They had no way of knowing. I'm sure you're just imagining things, Mr. Jefferson," she said lightly, not even considering getting back on the bus.

Jefferson shook his head. "Gal, I ain't foolin' with you. Go on now and get back on the bus."

She decided she had better take a firm hand with him. She had become used to working with elderly people from a job she held near the college at the Martin Luther King convalescent center for

25

the elderly. Old people had a bad habit of getting bossy in their old age. Now here was this fool trying to order her back on the bus after she had endured that bumpy overnight ride.

Henrietta wasn't very tall, but she had a way of carrying herself, and walking proud. She was slim, on the border of being skinny, yet she filled out the brown pants outfit she wore to perfection. Proud and haughty, that was the opinion of the men who watched her with interest.

"By God," Sonny-Boy Jones began, "that fuckin' bitch is still stuck-up as hell! Gets off the bus like she owns this here town, sees us sittin' here, then got the uppity not to speak!"

"Aw naw, Sonny. What you expect?" the short, muscular Earl Mason stated. Earl didn't bat an eye as Sonny turned on him. He stared into Sonny's cold, fish-like pale blue eyes and continued. "The gal witnessed the death of her pa before she left, so why the hell should she speak to some of the people she thinks killed him?" The breeze blew Earl's hair down in his face. He took his hand and pushed the reddish mass back out of his brown eyes.

Old man Turner, the owner of the general store, came out the door carrying a jug. "Yeah," he began, drawing the word out, making sure he held everybody's attention before he began to speak. "That old black gal done filled out a little since leavin'. Looks like she been eatin' wherever she been."

As the group of men watched and waited, old man Turner took his time about uncorking the jug. Every eye on the porch followed his motion as he tilted the jug up, swinging it over his forearm for support, and let the furious, burning corn likker run down his throat like water. When he brought the jug back down, he patted his huge belly.

"A'llllll," Turner groaned, "that's how you can tell good likker. It hits you in the gut."

"It seems to me it'll be kind of hard for anything to miss that goddamn gut you got, Turner," Earl stated as the rest of the men on the bench broke out laughing.

Before the anger rising in Turner's eyes could explode, Earl reached over and took the jug out of the man's hand. He knew from past experience that the store owner would take the jug back inside and not give any away if he thought for a moment that they were trying to make fun of him. Turner liked to talk. It made him feel important, and the only way he could hold an audience was to furnish the free whiskey. As long as the whiskey lasted, they would listen to his pompous sermons about other people.

Earl used one hand to push back the red-eyed store owner, while with the other he turned up the jug and took a big swig out of it.

While this was going on, the people still inside the bus peered out the windows at the strange looking hillbillies. Of course the men on the porch knew they were being watched, and many came in to town at just the times the bus arrived so that they could strut and pose in front of the foreigners. Anyone who didn't live near them was considered either a Yankee or a foreigner. Very rarely would one of the passengers get out of the bus and stretch his legs in the strange little town.

It was something old man Turner had never imagined, that the group of men loitering on his porch drove away potential customers. The people who might had gotten off and bought some candy or a paperback novel lost their desire after one look at the hangers-on. The group of men smelled of trouble. Anything was better than nothing, and whatever broke the boredom was considered fun.

As the bus driver came out of the general store, the sheriff came out beside him. The sheriff was stooped over from age, and his face had lines and wrinkles that matched his whiskey-ravished bloodshot eyes. Some of the people on the bus let out sighs of relief at the sight of the sheriff and bus driver. They knew it wouldn't be long now before they would be away from this country town.

"Well, Ed," the driver said to the sheriff, "maybe I'll see you nex' week when I'm due back through here. Anyhow, I'll tell Marge I saw you," he said, referring to his wife, who also happened to be the sheriff's only child.

The loitering men fell silent, listening, with the hope of picking up some idle gossip—something they could pass on to the people in the backwoods who didn't come to town often because they were too busy trying to earn a living out of the farms they worked. Only the shiftless, lazy, good-for-nothings hung out on the porch daily.

Two men started bear wrestling as the bus driver raced his motor once before slipping it into gear and pulling away. The other men let out loud yells, anything that might draw a fleeting moment of attention to themselves.

"By God, Sonny-Boy, there must have been an accident over at y'all's place, or somethin'?" the sheriff inquired.

"Why hell, naw. I can't cotton to why you'd say that, sheriff," Sonny-Boy answered, as his eyes followed the now fast moving bus. In another moment it would be taking the right hand turn and disappear. For some reason, Sonny always felt funny whenever he saw the bus leave. Maybe it was because of his dream. He had never told anybody, but it was his ambition to one day take a ride on that bus. Just to see where it went. In all his twenty-five years, he had never been over twenty-five miles away from his home. He had been deep in the swamp, but that didn't count. He had never seen a large city, other than on television. And television was a rarity. To see one, you had to visit one of the large farmers on one of the plantations, then hope he invited you to watch the electronic miracle.

"Why would I say it?" Sheriff Ed Bradford repeated. "Why it's just common sense, that's all. Your brothers Zeke and Jamie, they ain't here. This is the first time I can remember they missed the bus comin'. Why, I can't even recall when they did that before. You boys always come out of that swamp, rain or shine, once a week for the comin' of the bus."

Seeing his younger brother getting in deeper than he wanted him to, Jake, the oldest brother, spoke up. "Them boys got a big order on some 'gator hides, Ed," Jake stated, as he removed a bag of tobacco from his shirt pocket and began to roll a cigarette with one hand. "Yeah, them boys ought to be knee deep in 'gator shit 'bout this time of day. They been gone since last night, so I figure they made a good kill, and stayed in the swamps skinning," the tall blond man stated, slowly rubbing the scar on his left cheek.

The sheriff had stated many times that if you wanted to find out if the Jones boys were lying, get Jake to tell it and watch and see if he didn't rub that old scar of his. If he did, you could bet your roll he was tellin' one of the damndest lies of his life!

The departure of the bus was not only watched by the men on the porch, but Jefferson watched it leave with a feeling of dread. Perspiration broke out on his forehead as he whirled around to Henrietta.

"You little fool!" he yelled angrily. "If'n you'd only listened, but you can't listen 'cause you done went and got too smart!"

"I'm sorry, Mr. Jefferson, that you feel that way. I was going to ask you to help me with my bags until we ran into George, but that's all right. I don't want to impose on you any longer," she stated arrogantly. Before she could snatch up her bags, he reached out and held one.

"Listen child," he said, and his voice sounded so hurt and serious that she stopped to listen. "You yourself know that something must have happened, or George would be here by now. Nothing natural would have held that boy up, so somethin' happened. Now I could offer you my room to stay in if you want it, but it'd be another week now before the bus comes back." She started to speak, but he held up his hand. "Them honkies got somethin' in mind, child, 'bout you. I say they been talkin' 'bout it ever since last night. Now, I'm too old. I'd only hold you back. But what you got to do is act like you leavin' for y'all's place, then when you get out on the road, cut across the field and run for Massah Wilson's plantation. Once you get there, ain't no white trash goin' pester you, 'cause Massah Wilson don't allow them on his property."

Henrietta listened quietly, then asked, "You don't want to help me carry my bags home then?"

Jefferson shook his head. "Gal, ain't you been hearing what I been sayin'? I can't help you out on that road when them night riders come down on us. Ain't nothin' I can do but die, and I just ain't ready for it yet. I'm askin' you to do what I say. Leave your bags with me, then take off like you goin' walk home. Without the bags slowin' you none, you might be able to get across the field before any of them realize you ain't going home.

That's your only chance, child. The only one you got!"

Without another word, she pushed the bags toward him and started walking. Jefferson watched her go, praying she would do like he said. It would make the night riders mad, but just maybe it would hold them animals off. They'd have to think twice about raiding the farm, if she ever got home. They'd be scheming for the next week on how to get to her—maybe even puttin' it off until it was time for her departure. Then all old man Ben and George would have to do would be figure out some way to get her to the bus without their being waylayed on the way. It could be done, even if they'd have to beg some of the other niggers from the plantations to come by and ride to town with her. That way, they would have a chance. The so-called night riders would think twice about tackling six or seven niggers armed with shotguns. But first things first. The girl would have to do like he suggested. She had a chance, if she'd only realize her danger. Jefferson stood and watched until Henrietta was out of sight, then turned to observe what was happening across the street.

The two white men on the porch gave Henrietta a good ten minute head start, just as Jefferson had hoped they would. Now all she had to do was follow his suggestion and everything would be all right. He stood in the same spot and watched the two white men walk past.

"Lord," he prayed, "this poo' nigga ain't never asked for much, so please Suh, just this time, let this one get away. Please Lord, give this one a chance!"

3

THE WARNING that Pa had given him stayed on George's mind as he left the swamp creek river beds and entered the fast flowing stream that led to the large main river. The one he now traveled was only fifty feet in width, with large grayish-green roots hanging out from the shore line on each side. Branches from the trees hung out over the water, so that he was constantly under the shade from the trees. He switched from pole to paddle.

If the Jones boys decided to stop him, it would come on the river, George realized. He ducked his head to miss some low-hanging vines, his eyes searching amongst them for death—death that could drop from the least expected place. Even here, out of the swamp, and on what these people called high ground, the creatures of death lurked.

Had he wanted to, George could have crossed over and used the much safer water route. There the long hanging vines had been cut to eliminate the danger of unwelcome snakes dropping down from the tree branches. If danger was to come, George reasoned, it would also strike from that side of the river. Whoever had been left behind to cut him off would lay on that side of the river.

The closer he came to his chosen spot to leave the dugout and go overland, the higher his hope began to climb. Since he was leaving the river much quicker than where they would think he'd depart, he had reason to think that they might have set their ambush too far up the river.

As the high hopes were beginning to soar in his mind, the crack of a rifle bullet, then the swift rush of air past his head, shattered them once and for all. He went over the side of the boat, making a big splash. He started swimming strongly for the near riverbank.

There were no other shots as he hugged the huge root of an old tree. The many roots coming out of the tall willow tree offered the best of cover. As he made his way out of the water there were no more shots. Whoever had taken the shot at him had meant it as a warning. They could have killed him if they had wanted to.

Even while he reached this conclusion, he still didn't take any changes. He stayed as close to cover as possible, moving through the wet ground on his stomach.

Across the way, Jamie shaded his eyes with his hand. "That goddamn coon is better than any cajun aroun', Zeke. He done disappeared, unless you hit him by mistake, boy."

"If'n I'd set out to hit him, you'd be seein' tha' nigga's ass floatin' on top of the water by now," Zeke replied, still holding the smoking gun at shoulder height.

"Well, where'd the niggra go? He can't be that good! I'd seen him come up huggin' one of them stumps over there, but I swear, Zeke, I ain't seen no sight of him since then."

"That's right, boy," Zeke replied. "Yo' ought to have been able to tell from the way he went over that weren't nothin' wrong with that niggra, but scared!"

The two brothers grinned at each other, then Zeke set his gun down and grabbed Jamie's waist and danced him around the small open space.

"I don't reckon that coon goin' stop runnin' 'til he reach the swamp," Jamie stated, after his brother finally released him. Again the two men stood and grinned at each other.

"Come on, boy, we better be gettin' on the way before Jake and Sonny-Boy tear up that little old black pussy!" Zeke stated as he bent to pick up the rifle. "I'm plannin' on it bein' us, Jamie, old boy. Yes indeedie, I ain't lettin' nobody bust that black puss 'til I done got me some of it."

"Hell, Zeke, she been gone way to school too long. Some big black buck done rode that mount, partner. What we goin' get is the leftovers. Hell's fire, boy! She'll be beggin' us to give it to her. Just like tha' old big black gal on Wilson's plantation. Shits fire, boy! All we got to do is send a whistle, and when she hears it, she comes arunnin' with her dress hiked up to her neck!"

"Uh huh. You just listen to old Zeke, boy. He knows what he's talkin' 'bout. This one ain't like that, I'm tellin' you. She thinks she's somethin' special. Always did. Walks like she got gold between them black thighs of hers, she does."

"I'll be willin' to bet you, Zeke, that old Jake can train this one to come to our whistle."

It took a minute before Zeke answered. He led the way quickly through the trees, following a narrow game path. "If'n it was any other one, I might think so, but this one's different. She too dark to have human blood, boy, but she carries herself like a white lady. Don't know why, neither.

Ain't never been able to figure that one out. Where the hell she got them lady ways, being swamp meat and all."

"Balls of fire, Zeke, all of 'em like that. That boy George speaks like he's a Yankee or somethin'. Don't talk like the rest of the coons 'round here."

"Likes them books, he do," Zeke replied. "I done seen him off in the swamp layin' up on the bank readin', ain't thinkin' nobody near for miles. Yeah, I done walked up on him a couple times, 'fore he could hide what he was doin'. Made him show me one of 'em one day. Jehovah's beard, goddamn words on the cover longer than my pecker!"

Without another word Zeke broke into a dog-trot, his long legs eating up the distance between him and his destination. Jamie ran easily at his heel. Both men blended well with their surroundings. Woodsmen, back country woodsmen, born too late in life for their skills to help them. A hundred years ago men like them went west and built empires.

The two men hurried toward the meeting that they knew would have to occur if the woman took the trail out of town that they expected her to take.

Henrietta, hurrying down the dirt road, came to the bend where she would have to cut across the field to reach the Wilson plantation. She stopped and gave the alternate route a fleeting thought, then continued on her way. It didn't have to be like the old man thought, she reasoned. If she hurried, she sincerely doubted that anything would happen.

Now that she had made up her mind, Henrietta didn't waste any time. With long strides she turned down the narrow pathway that would eventually come to the river where she expected to find George. If he wasn't there, there were always plenty of dugouts laying around. She hadn't forgotten how to paddle one. There was another choice. She could walk the long way home, if she stayed on the road, but she was sure George wouldn't come that way. So she decided to cut through the heavy wooded section that led down to the river.

Henrietta was halfway to the river when she heard someone approaching from that direction. Whoever it was was in a hurry. She immediately assumed it was George, hurrying to meet her. She smiled to herself. In a way, she had let that old man get to her. She had worried over nothing, all because an old man had seen a ghost behind every tree. In this day and age, things just didn't happen like they used to. Of course her father had been killed, but today, they couldn't commit a murder like that and get away with it.

With that thought in mind, she rounded a curve in the forest and came face to face with two of the men who had killed her father!

Oh my God, she thought. Of all the people to have to meet, she couldn't have wished for anybody worse than the Jones boys. She despised the whole family, including their sister who she had attended school with before leaving. The one-room school on the Wilson's plantation was for both black and white—poor white anyway. Most of the whites kept their kids out of the free school because blacks went there. They'd rather not have an education for their kids than to have to admit to friends that their child was attending school with niggers. It just wasn't done.

For some reason the Jones kids had been different. Their mother had forced them to go. Rather than grow up totally ignorant, she swallowed her pride and sent her youngest kids off to the one-room school with the blacks. The result being that now the Jones boys and sister were one of the few rural whites who could actually read. The rest were dependent upon friends and neighbors whenever something came to them through the mail. They'd have to take it around until they found someone to read it for them.

"Well, I'll be damn! Look what's lookin' for us!" Jamie cried out as Henrietta took a backwards step. Oh my God, she cried out silently, it's true then! Everything the old man tried to warn me against, only I was too foolish to pay heed!

"If you gentlemen don't mind, would you allow me to pass?" The small trail through the woods was only wide enough for one person. More than that had to travel in single file.

"My God, yes, let the lady by, boy," Zeke said and stepped back against one of the trees.

As Henrietta started to go past, he reached out and grabbed her by her small waist. "Come here, gal, let me see what's under them fancy clothes!" With that, he reached around her and tore the white blouse off her shoulders. The coat that matched the pants suit she wore had been carried in the crook of her arm. Now, as she struggled to get free, she dropped it.

"Please, please," she begged, struggling in vain. All my fault, my fault, the thought kept flashing through her mind.

Jamie came up and grabbed the bra she wore. He pulled it down until it was around her stomach. "The hell with it, she won't be needin' this stuff no ways," he said, and tore the rest of her blouse completely off.

She still struggled in Zeke's arms, but it was to no avail. No matter how she tried, she couldn't break the man's grip. If anything, her wiggling and squirming only aroused him. He could feel his dick begin to harden.

"By God, Zeke, look at them tits on her, will you?" Jamie stated, taking one of them in his hand and squeezing it until she cried out. "I ain't seen none like that in some time, I'll tell yo' boy. Them critters stand right on up there!"

"Damn them tits," Zeke cried out, spit running out of the corners of his mouth, and dropping down on the half naked woman. He reached around him and ran his hand down the front of her pants, playing in the tightly curled hairs he found there.

"George, George," she cried out in vain. "Please, George, help!" she screamed, now thoroughly frightened. This can't be happening, not to me, she prayed. But even as she did this she could feel the hands all over her. This couldn't be what she had saved herself for. No, not this. Not like an animal, taken in the woods like a dog in heat. *No*, she dragged the scream out. Then she heard people coming. Help was on the way. She felt relieved. She had known God couldn't have forsaken her

like this. No, she was too honest. Too true to the
faith. God would never desert her, even here in the
back woods. As the people came closer she stopped
struggling. Then the men came around the bend.
Piss began to run down her leg. For the first time
in her adult life, she had wet on herself. Oh my
God, she cried. Lord, have you forsaken one of
your flock? She cried out in her despair, for the
help she had heard coming turned out to be the
other two Jones brothers.

"Well now, Zeke, what you done went and
found yourself, boy?" Jake yelled out as they
came rushing up to the two men struggling with
the girl. "It looks like you boys could use some
help," he said, as he grabbed one of her tender
young breasts and brutally handled it. There was
no tenderness in the man's caress, only animal lust.
They slobbered on themselves, spit running down
their chins, as each man fought the other to get
different holds on the woman.

Finally she could feel herself being dragged
down to the ground. Rough hands tore her pants
off her body, until she lay naked under the
branches of the tall willow tree. Birds flew overhead, calling out to each other, but Henrietta heard
nothing, as she felt fingers being rammed up inside
her body. She called out, screamed for mercy,

begged and promised, but to no avail. The men didn't hear. Her panic meant nothing to them. They were beyond stopping. Their only desire now was lust.

4

GEORGE SLIPPED THE HEAVY BOOTS OFF, then removed his shirt and tied it around his shoes. Now, he was ready—he believed he had waited long enough. His ambushers should have gone long ago, if their plans for Henrietta were still in force.

The dugout was out of reach but that was a small matter. He didn't have to have a boat to get across the fifty foot creek. George waded into the water until it came up to his chin, then started to swim. He made sure he didn't splash loudly, not out of fear of the men who had shot at him, but just in case one of the alligators from the swamp might have taken a notion and come this far up river. It had happened in the past, and he wasn't taking any chances. To meet one of the creatures out in the middle of the creek would spell big trouble.

He swam with care, making each stroke count until he reached the other side. He cut through the heavily wooded section until he came to the tiny path that led away from the river. Sometimes he ran, other times he walked briskly until his wind came back, and then he'd break out and start tracking again. I must pace myself, he warned himself. But in his haste, he found himself running at top speed until he was completely spent.

The thought that everything was his fault kept flashing through his mind with each step he took. Finally he had to stop and lean against a tree until he could catch his wind. Tears of despair rolled freely down his cheeks.

Even if he hurried he knew now that he would be too late. It had taken him too long to walk through the woods. With a boat he would have been there. The thought that nothing could really happen to his sister was no more than a young boy's foolish dream. He had seen them murder his father, so why wouldn't the rednecks misuse his sister if they felt like it.

Then, suddenly he heard a nerve shattering scream. The desperate cry soared through the forest until he had to put his hands against his ears to blot out the sound. Then slowly he began to make his way toward the noise. The closer he got, the more cautious he became. He moved on the tips of his toes, knowing that if he was discovered, death would be his lot.

As soon as he thought he was near enough to them, he got down on his knees and began to crawl. He moved slowly, pushing sticks out of his way that would have cracked under his weight.

The screams became even more nerve-racking as he drew nearer. Stretched out on his stomach, he reached out and shoved aside the remaining bushes. The sight that greeted him was so shocking that he closed his eyes tightly, trying not to see what he could hear all too well.

Henrietta struggled against the overwhelming odds while two of the brothers stood back and laughed. Only the youngest two, Sonny-Boy and Jamie, wrestled with the woman. She kicked out at them and tried to use her nails, but it was to no avail. Her thin white blouse was ripped from her back, and then came her bra. Being half-naked in front of the white men drove her to a frenzy. She screamed and scratched like some wild animal. There was no thought of surrender.

After receiving a deep scratch down the right side of his face, Jamie, screaming like a woman, struck out wildly with his fist and knocked Henrietta off her feet and onto her back. Sonny-Boy bent down and jerked her pants down to her knees.

"Hot doggie," Sonny-Boy yelled, and followed it up with a rebel yell as he leaned down and snatched her mini panties down. But before he could get them completely off, Henrietta regained her senses and began struggling frantically.

At the sight of her pubic hairs, Jamie let out a cry of lust and threw himself down, and pinned her arms. "Get 'em off, Sonny, get 'em off," he ordered breathlessly as he felt his penis becoming hard and stiff.

"Goddamn it, she won't stop kickin'," Sonny yelled as he tried to get the panties completely off the woman. Finally he knelt down on one of her legs and pushed the other one as wide as he could get it. But this didn't work, because now the pants were stretched and just became tighter.

"By God, fuck all that crap," Jake stated as he strolled over. He took out his long Bowie knife and reached down and cut the garments free from the woman's legs. He grinned as he narrowly missed being kicked in the face as he stepped back from his handiwork.

The sounds of her cries stung George until he had to fight back the madness that was about to overcome him. If only he had brought along the shotgun. Even if he had had to resort to strength to take it from the old man, that would have been better than what he was hearing. He refused to open his eyes. The guilt lay on him heavily, each scream was printed in his memory.

Jamming his finger as far into the woman as he could, Jamie let out a cry of bewilderment. "By God, we done got hold to a real virgin!"

"It ain't a nigger bitch this side of heaven as old as her and still a virgin. Niggers just don't practice things like that which you could expect from a white woman," Jake said loudly, sneering as if his words had to be the truth.

Jake moved closer to the struggling woman and, as Jamie removed his hand, he tried to ram three fingers into the woman at once. "Goddamn it," he retorted, "this is some of the tightest pussy I ever played with." He continued to force his fingers inside the woman until two of them went in. Pushing hard and deep, he grinned evilly as she screamed out in pain. As he removed his fingers, blood gushed out from where he had busted the maidenhead. He stared down at her bleeding cunt as if it was some rare jewel that he had just discovered.

After that, Henrietta made up her mind to stop trying to fight them off, and to save her strength so

51

that one day she would be able to testify against the four brothers.

Sonny-Boy stepped back with a frown on his face. It was quite evident that he didn't have any stomach for the bloody pussy. "By God," he growled, "I ain't about to stick my pecker in no butchered hog, you can bet on it."

Henrietta gave a sigh of relief. She prayed that the others would feel the same way. Maybe staying a virgin would pay off after all. She remembered the times back at college when she went to the dances so happily. But after a while the word had spread that she wouldn't fuck. None of the black brothers wanted to waste their time on a black woman whom you couldn't even lay unless you married her.

Even as she prayed with her eyes closed, Jamie was quickly disrobing himself. His shirt came off first, then the overalls, until he wore only a dirty pair of gray underwear with the sleeves and legs cut off.

Jamie didn't bother to remove his underwear. He pulled out his small four inch belly button dick and jumped down between the woman's outstretched legs. He ignored the blood as he pumped up and down, grunting like a pig in heat.

"Ride 'em, cowboy," Jake yelled excitedly. His

shallow face was flushed, and the scar on his left cheek began to glow as if too much blood was rushing to his head.

None of the others bothered to watch the oldest brother. Zeke pulled out his prick and began to masturbate.

"What the hell you doin' that for?" Sonny-Boy inquired as his eyes narrowed down to tiny slits as he observed his older brother.

"So that I can," his voice came in gasps as he tried to answer while reaching a climax. The sperm spurted out in a long arc, only a small amount got on his hand. He rubbed it off on his pants leg, then answered his brother. "I wanna stay with that black pussy for a while, Sonny. Don't you know if you jerk off first, you can damn near hump all night after that?"

With a sudden yell, Jamie gave a shrill scream not unlike the sound a woman would make, and tried to roll off the woman. "Goddamn," he roared, "this bitch is stiffer than my damn pecker was." He slowly lifted himself up from between the woman's legs. Blood was spattered down the front of his underwear, but he paid no heed to it. "Ain't no fun in no cunt this cold, boys. Looks like we done wasted our time."

Sonny-Boy shook his long shaggy hair out of his

eyes and kicked Henrietta viciously in the side. She yelled loudly, but remained on her back. The sight of his brother jerkin' off had aroused Sonny-Boy more than the sight of the woman being fucked by Jamie.

"Now hold your horses there!" Jake, the oldest of the four men ordered. "There's more than one way to skin a cat. I been plannin' on this old gal for some time, so just hold up on that roughness." He spoke in a slow drawl. He was used to being obeyed by the rest of his clan.

Sonny dropped his eyes, not able to meet his oldest brother's glance. He had been clubbed down too many times in the past to try arguing with Jake.

The three men watched as Jake removed an old army canteen he had tossed down beside an old tree stump. "I told you boys I was goin' stump break this here filly, and I meant every word of it," Jake stated coldly as he walked over toward the woman. His eyes glittered dangerously as he knelt down beside her.

From the bushes where he hid, George finally opened his eyes and glanced at the scene. Since he hadn't heard any screams, his young mind tried to figure out what Jake had in store for his sister. He shivered at the thought of what the scum out there could do.

Henrietta never noticed Jake next to her as she kept her eyes closed and prayed. The first one hadn't been too bad, so she believed she could come through it without too much damage. If she wasn't hurt too much, she decided to try and keep the rape from George. He was too young, and it might mess his mind up for good. Oh, Father in heaven, she prayed, it's only my body they abuse, so help me to have the strength to overcome this day.

"What's that you got there, Jake? I hope you ain't 'bout to waste no good corn likker on her," Zeke stated as he kept his knee down on her right arm and rubbed her bare breasts with his other hand. "I'd thought she'd have bigger tits than these little bastards." He swore as he continued to rub her breasts roughly.

Jake rubbed the scar on his left cheek and gave his brothers a grotesque grin. "Ain't you country boys ever heard 'bout a little Spanish fly? It's somthin' they use down Texas way when they want to breed some stock."

"By God, Jake," Zeke yelled happily, "if you got some of that there stuff, I'll bet a fatman against a pile of shjt it'd take some of the stiffness out of her ass!"

Jake grinned, leaned down and lifted up her head. "One of you boys force her mouth open so we can get it down," he ordered.

Jamie quickly bent down and squeezed her cheeks together, forcing her to open up her mouth. Jake poured the Spanish fly down her throat. Henrietta tried to spit it up, but the men weren't having any of that. They made her hold it down and swallow all of it.

"How much of it is you supposed to give her?" Jamie asked.

Jake shook her head. "Damned if I know. But I reckon there's enough in this canteen to fix her up. The fellow who sold it to me said it was enough there to make a bull handle a pasture full of heffers."

"Aw shit, boy, it ain't a woman born we four couldn't satisfy, Jamie, so quit your worryin'," Zeke answered loudly.

"She ain't nothin' but a fuckin' nigga wench anyway, so who gives a shit," Sonny-Boy stated.

It suddenly occurred to George that he just might have enough time to run home and get the shotgun and come back. It was sure he couldn't help her without some kind of weapon, and the men in the pasture had their guns laid out in such a way that it would have been impossible to belly up and steal one. The gun that had belonged to George's father stood in the clearing shining brightly. George turned his head away. There was a good probability that the gun had been the real reason for his father's death. The tall, lanky Zeke had wanted it from the first time he had set eyes on it. Zeke had even come over and tried to borrow it. But his father knew that the cracker had no intention of ever returning it.

So when George's father refused to loan out the gun, the anger on the cracker's part became open hatred. He refused to take the crackers seriously. He had confidence in his rifle, and he didn't mind using it on a few hillbillies if they crowded him.

Instead of getting up and going for the shotgun, George lay there, speculating over it. The sweat ran off his stern features, yet he couldn't make up his mind what to do.

It was just like the night of his father's death. The cold ball of fear clutched at his gut, yet the fear was not for himself, it was for someone he loved. He was again overcome by how helpless he was.

Tears ran down his cheeks as he remembered. Coming out of the outhouse he had seen the white men. Instead of running and hiding when they called out to him, he had approached them slowly.

The men had grabbed him, and used him to get his father out of the cabin unarmed—something he would never have done, except for his son. He had tossed out his rifle on the promise that the boy would be released. Once the gun was out and on the ground the men had released George, who fled to the cabin where his father met him at the door and embraced him for the last time. Even as his father held him, one of the crackers came up and clubbed his father in the head with the stock of an old shotgun.

His father fell to the ground, and his grandfather came out and pulled the boy away. George had wanted to try and help his father. They dragged his father away from the cabin to the nearest tree. George watched from behind his grandfather's legs as Zeke tossed a rope over a branch and caught the noose when it came back down.

"Go in the house, boy!" his grandfather had ordered, but George didn't budge. He stood there and watched as the men tied his father's arms tightly behind him, then Jake fitted the noose around the man's neck.

A sharp scream from the doorway caused all the men to turn around. Henrietta came charging out of the cabin. She was only a child at the time, so the men spared her life. They only disarmed her, then kicked her viciously in the ass and shoved her toward the grandfather with the stern order, "Gramps, you better teach them young niggas some respect, or we'll do it for you."

The old man stood there with tears running down his cheeks, tightly clutching the two children to him. They could feel the old man shaking as he watched his only son being strung up. No sound came from him, but the kids could feel him shake uncontrollably.

"By God, we just oughta cut this smart ass nigger's nuts off first!" Zeke yelled, waiting to see how the other men took to his notion.

Earl, a short muscular white man who owned his own land, snorted loudly. "The hell you say, Zeke. This done got way past what it was supposed to be now." Some of the corn whiskey he had drunk earlier began to wear off. "All you'd mentioned at the bar was comin' out and givin' this coon a good whippin', now 'stead of that, I see you and your brother had other ideas from the start. If I'd known this was goin' to be a hangin', this is one redneck who wouldn't be here now."

The other white men hooted and yelled, "Well, I'll be dang damn blasted," Jake snorted loudly. "If I didn't know better, I'd say old Red is a coon lover."

Earl, who was called Red by most of the men because of the color of his hair, only glared around. "You boys can say what you damn please, but this old boy ain't done nothin' that I know of that should give us reason to hang him, let alone cut his balls off."

Willie, a tall slim man with a shallow face, leered around at the group of men. He was a cruel man by nature, disappointed in life, knowing he would never be anything but a handyman to be used by whatever redneck had the money to hire him. He hated niggers with a passion. To him, they were all animals and needed to be dead. One reason for his hatred was that he had to work in the fields right beside them, knowing that they were earning the same money that he was. The knowledge only served to pour coal on the open fire of his hatred.

"Ain't the way I heard it, Red!" Willie growled. "The boys said we was goin' lynch us a coon 'fore daybreak. Only reason I come along." He reached over and grabbed hold of the rope and began to pull on it so that the black man with the noose around his neck had to stand on his tiptoes.

Not wanting Earl to ruin his necktie party, Jake grabbed the rope and helped Willie pull on it. So as not to miss out on the fun, Zeke joined his brother, and before the shocked eyes of the little

60

boy and girl, the three men hung the tall, husky, black man.

As these bitter reflections crossed his mind, it also occurred to the young boy that these men might kill his sister when they finished abusing her. Just as he made up his mind to go for the shotgun, the Spanish fly the men had given to Henrietta began to take effect. The transformation was so shocking that George was rooted to his place of concealment. At first he couldn't believe his eyes, as he watched with a growing horror. The spectacle in front of him was inconceivable. The woman he was now watching couldn't be his sister, for what he now saw was a shrieking, sex crazy woman whose face was contorted in a hideous mask of lust. He became filled with a deep sense of disgust and revulsion.

5

THE DRUG THE MEN GAVE HENRIETTA hit her suddenly. It was as if all her nerves began craving the same thing at once. Her vagina became a burning flame—a fire that was about to consume her. She began writhing in the throes of an uncontrollable anguish. She lay on the ground squirming, moaning, while she rubbed the sides of her vagina viciously. There was no tenderness, no attempt to build up to masturbating on her part. It was as if an acid had been tossed on her sexual parts, and she was trying to rub it off.

Sonny-Boy grinned wickedly. "I wanna give it to you, Jake, old boy. You sure as hell took the stiffness out of her ass!" Even as he spoke, he removed his pants and shirt, revealing the same kind of underwear his brothers wore. He took his time undressing, answering each joke one of his brothers tossed at him with one of his own as he got completely naked.

"That old boy don't wanna get his drawers dirty," Zeke said, grinning broadly. "You reckon you can handle it, boy?"

"I don't reckon I got to jerk off first," Sonny-Boy answered sharply as he dropped down on one knee.

Before he could move any farther, she had reached up and got him around the neck and pulled him down on top of herself. Her fingers searched wildly for his prick, and finding it, she instantly raised up and vigorously forced it inside of herself.

"Goddamn," Sonny-Boy groaned, as it dawned on him that he was the one being raped. She held him tightly, too tightly, and when he began to reach his climax her grip was so tight that he could not enjoy it. "Turn loose, gal, Goddamn it," he growled angrily.

Instead of turning him loose, Henrietta tightened

her grip and rolled her pelvic bone against him brutally. He groaned from the pain, and struggled to break free.

Jake nodded his head at Zeke. "Get ready boy, you're next. This old gal ain't in the mood for waitin', so we goin' start breakin' her in right!" He waited until his brother had undressed, then held the man back. "Just hold on, bro," he ordered the naked man.

Zeke stood waiting, undecided, not knowing which way to go. He made a sorry sight standing buck naked in the clearing. His skin was dirty white, spotted with patches of yellowish hair. It was as if his body had never seen the sunlight. It was pale like a fish that had stayed out of the water too long.

"You stay right here, Zeke!" Jake ordered sharply, then walked over and helped Sonny-Boy break loose from the struggling woman. Jamie was no help at all, he was rolling on the ground laughing, holding his sides, and pointing at Sonny-Boy.

As soon as Sonny-Boy got free, Jake pinned the woman to the ground with his foot on her chest. As she reached up for his groin, he reached down and slapped her viciously across the face.

"Now you listen close, gal, if'en you goin' be

wantin' some more of these old peckers, you listen real close. When I walk back across the clearing, you wait until I whistle like this," and he demonstrated for her. "Now gal, that's the only way you goin' be able to get some of this white dick, you understand?"

Henrietta didn't really understand. At that point she was just about out of her mind. The only thing she could think about was putting out the fire inside of her. The burning, the craving, the desire was eating her up. She started to crawl across the clearing where Jake had gathered all the men. They stood sipping on corn likker as they watched her.

As she started to crawl, Jake shook his finger at her. "Gal, you ain't payin' 'tention to your teacher, 'cause I ain't whistled yet."

He might as well have been talking to the trees, or the birds that continued to fly overhead, because they may have paid more heed to what he was saying that Henrietta. She had only one thought and desire, and that was to reach the naked man. The sight of the worm-like penis hanging down drove her on. Something told her that the small object that hung down could bring her the temporary relief she sought. If only for a brief moment, anything would be better than the consuming fire inside of her. Maybe he could put it out. Fuck, fuck, fuck, the thought flashed through her mind. It was the only way, the only thing that she cared about.

"I reckon it's too soon," Jake said more to himself than to his brothers standing around him. He whistled sharply anyway before she reached them.

Zeke rubbed on his penis as he watched the woman draw closer. His dick was curved to the right, as if the use of his right hand had fixed the curve in it. Masturbation, or too much tender handling made it what men called a handmade dick.

"Go on, boy," Jake ordered. "I know you don't get much pussy, Zeke, ol' coon. Black or white, you just ain't been gettin' your rightful 'mount of nookie."

The laughter of the three men meant nothing to the couple as they met in the clearing. Zeke was beyond caring about his brothers' ridicule. Jake had been right, he was a shy man, so he didn't get much pussy. The white women wouldn't look at him, and he was too scared to go around the black plantations by himself at night, seeking out the black women who would have anything to do with a white man for a price. One of the reasons was that his family was what they called dirt poor, and many of the plantation blacks had more than Zeke's people, so he didn't have anything to bargain with.

With Jake it was different. The blacks feared him. Whenever he appeared around them, you could see the fear in their eyes. Some of them actually trembled outright, shaking in their shoes. So Jake was able to go through the plantations and fuck at will, picking and choosing like the old masters of the plantation used to do.

As the woman's arms went around him, Zeke felt as if this time it really was different. This was the first time that a woman really wanted him. He could feel himself coming instantly, but unlike Sonny-Boy, the tight grip of Henrietta's arms around his waist made him feel wanted, so instead of trying to break loose as she raised up and rubbed her pelvic bone against him, trying desperately to feel his penis inside her, he pressed down, meeting her demand with his demand. He stayed with her until his penis got hard again and continued to fuck. The hooting and hollering of his brothers only spurred him on, but even with his desire he wasn't enough for Henrietta. She wore him down, then demanded more, until he was completely drained. Even then she wouldn't release him, continuing to hold him tightly.

From his place of concealment George began to back out until he was sure he was far enough away before he stopped crawling. Then he slowly climbed to his feet and began to run. Most of the time he ran blindly, because of the flow of tears that ran down his cheeks. He had seen them give her something, true enough, but whatever they gave her couldn't have made her act like that unless she wanted to. Henrietta just liked being fucked by crackers, that's all. He couldn't face it any other way.

When he reached the river he searched up and down the banks until he found a dugout hidden behind some trees. He pushed it slowly down the moss-covered bank until he reached the water. His movements had slowed up quite a bit since leaving the path in the woods. There was no need for urgency, he reasoned. She acted as if she liked what was happening. In fact, she was begging for it, couldn't get enough.

George wasn't a virgin himself. Some nights he went down to the Wilson's plantation and put on the dog. The young girls down there liked to see him. He had taken his share of them out in the woods, or to somebody's empty cabin, so he knew what it was all about. When a woman wanted it she would ask for it, it she wanted it bad enough.

But no matter how much he talked about it to himself, he still thought about the drink they gave her. Spanish fly, Jake had called it. He had never heard of it himself, but to his young mind, he couldn't imagine anything making a woman act like Henrietta was acting.

He picked up the paddle as he jumped in the boat and began to row. The more he thought about it, the more unsure he became. This was something he'd have to take up with grandpa. It was too big for him to figure out himself.

Before George reached home, the shadows of evening were moving over the swamp land. In a matter of minutes it would be so dark that a man wouldn't be able to see his hand in front of him. George had taken his time getting home, thinking that there was no rush. He was so naive that he really believed his sister was enjoying herself.

When he turned into the lane that led toward their home he could see his grandfather standing down by the water waiting. Before he poled in to the dry land, his grandfather called out.

"Boy, where's your sister at?" The old man stood there watching his grandchild closely, his eyes unreadable in the evening light.

George hung his head, he didn't know where to

begin. "Gramps, them Jones boys was waitin' on her. It wasn't nothin' I could do, you kept the shotgun."

The boy's words stung the old man. He turned away, not wanting the boy to see the hurt in his eyes. "Boy, if'en you'd had the gun, do you think you could have did much?" Before George could reply, the old man spun on his heel and marched toward the cabin. George was pulling the dugout up on dry land when the old man returned, the shotgun cradled under his arm. When he reached the dugout, he removed an old pistol from under his coat.

"I can't see too well no more, boy, so you may have to use this while I count on old Bessie here." He patted the old shotgun affectionately.

"Gramps," George began, then didn't know how to explain to the old man what he wanted to say. He hesitated, then just rushed into it. "Gramps, what them Jones boys is doing to her, is something she seems to like." From the look the old man tossed his way, he hurriedly added, "I mean, they gave her something to drink, then she just stopped yellin' and actin' like a good woman."

The old man shot the young boy a blistering stare, then inquired, "Boy you wouldn't by chance know what it was them crackers gave her, would you?"

George glanced at the water as he pushed the paddle down and poled slowly in the direction he had just come from. "It was somethin' old Jake called Spanish fly."

For one of the few times in his life, George heard his grandfather curse in front of him. "Boy," he roared, "are you sure that's what they said they were goin' give her?"

All George could do was nod his head. The sound of his grandfather's voice frightened him. He had never seen him like this before, not even on the night his father was hung. Could he have only read his grandfather's mind he would have truly been frightened, because the old man had become fed up. This was the last straw as far as he was concerned. His children were raised now and his duty was over.

When he watched his only son die, he had held back for the children's sake, or he would have died beside his son that night. But someone had to live to take care of the small children. Now his job was finished. He believed that George could survive without him. Now he had to go and see about Henrietta, and if killing was necessary he would do it. His only regret was that he hadn't made up his mind earlier when the boy first came home. None of this should have happened. It was all his fault.

"Boy, get this thing to movin'. We ain't got all day!" the old man ordered as he glanced around for a paddle. He laid the shotgun down as he picked up the other paddle, using his whole body. He worked at it with a smooth motion, and from his actions you could see where the young boy had learned from. They moved swiftly down the river now, with both men working together. Even so, darkness fell on them before they were halfway there.

Back in the clearing in the woods, the men grew tired of their game. Each man had had the woman over two times, some even three or more. They were worn out, yet she was still craving more and more affection from them.

Jake, who had long ago trained her to come when he whistled, stared at her coldly. "Well, boys, I reckon we done about played out, wouldn't you say?" He glanced around at his brothers. "Anybody else want another piece of ass before we go?" he inquired sharply.

Sonny-Boy shook his head as he picked up his shotgun. "I don't reckon nobody wants none, Jake. What you reckon we ought to do with her?" he asked, pointing the gun in her direction. There was no doubt in anybody's mind what Sonny was thinking. He wanted to kill the woman.

"Hold on there, boy," Jake said lightly. "Ain't goin' be none of that. What for you think I went through all the trouble of stump breakin' that young filly for? Not for you to blow no fuckin' hole through her with your shotgun!"

"Well, what the hell we goin' do with her then?" Sonny asked, his voice breaking into a whine.

"Don't worry about it," Jake replied as he walked over and picked up his rifle. "Somebody from her family should be coming along soon huntin' for her. They know we're about finished with her."

"Hell for, Jake," Jamie cried out. "You reckon they know we been coverin' this ol' gal?"

"Hell yes, boy. The way she been calowildin' earlier, 'fore we got her settled down. You can bet your ass some nigger heard her, but just had enough sense not to come runnin' in on us spoilin' our fun," Jake answered as he put the gun in the crook of his arm.

"I don't like that crap," Jamie answered slowly as he picked up his old shotgun.

"It ain't 'bout what you like or not, boy!" Jake stated coldly as he took one last glance around the clearing. "I reckon we can go on our way now," he said, and gave his brothers a wolfish grin. Without another glance at the crazed woman, he led his brothers down the path that would eventually lead them back to town.

6

THE EARLY EVENING MOONLIGHT was the only thing that witnessed the bereaved woman's antics. When the men left, she had crawled after them, until the last one in the rear had kicked her viciously in the face. Now, as blood ran freely from her nose, she still crawled around on all fours, moaning like some sick animal. Her eyes searched the clearing, looking for something she could use to still the burning inside of her. She noticed something that resembled a long stick near the pathway. As she made her way toward it, the stick began to move. She hurried, trying to overtake it, but like a drunk, luck was in her favor, because the slow moving death that she chased slithered under some brush and out of her sight. In the darkness she couldn't make out which bush it had gone under, so as death waited coiled, she went past it.

Finally she spotted a long stick and this time it did not crawl away. She picked up the long dead branch and leaned against a tree. Slowly Henrietta began to push the long stick up inside of herself, as she moaned loudly. The relief she sought didn't come, but she continued to try, forcing the stick deeper and deeper.

With George leading the way, the two men came to the clearing on the run. It had been hard on the old man, but he had managed to keep up with the pace the young man had set ever since leaving the boat. When they reached the clearing, they could hear a woman crying, but couldn't see her in the dark. When the old man finally saw her leaning back against the tree, his heart went out to her. He at once saw what she was trying to do.

When George saw what she was doing, he blushed down to his shoetops and turned away, sickened at the sight. The old man glanced at him angrily. "What would you have her do, boy, kill herself while you looked away?" the old man said as he rushed forward and tried to pry her hands loose from the stick.

"Now take it easy, gal, Grandaddy is here now,

so don't worry about a thing," he said lightly, still trying to make her release the stick. How much has she got in her, he wondered silently, as he forced her hands away from it.

Henrietta didn't even recognize her grandfather as she glanced up at the old man. The only thing he represented at the time was a man, a person who had that certain thing that would stop the burning inside of her.

Just as suddenly as a snake, she released the stick and went for his crotch. The old man let out a grunt of pain as she grabbed his testicles.

"Boy!" The word exploded from him. "Help me, boy!" It was an order. Without the boy's help, the old man wouldn't have been able to handle the young woman himself. She was beyond control and force was the only thing that would help her at this point.

With George's help, they were able to break her grip on the old man's private parts. Before they could think, she attacked George, trying to pull his penis free. Before he knew what was happening, she had torn his blue jeans loose, busting the buttons as she snatched wildly at what she sought.

"Hold her, boy," grandfather groaned. "I got to find some kind of vine so we can tie her." He set off through the woods in search of what he needed. It took a while before he found the right kind, using his Bowie knife to cut enough loose. The old man's heart beat wildly. There was too much strain on it and he was pushing it too hard. He had to stop and lean against a tree for a moment, then he forced himself to continue. Spots appeared before his eyes, but he only blinked and tried to go on. Stumbling, and just barely moving faster than a walk, he made his way back. When he reached the clearing he had to stop and lean against a tree again.

"Hurry, Gramps," George yelled, not noticing the condition of his grandfather.

The old man knew he couldn't walk any farther, so he dropped down on all fours and began to crawl. It was then that George noticed that the old man was in bad shape, but there was nothing he could do about it at that moment. His sister was all he could handle. His pants were down around his hips, and since he didn't wear any underclothes, his long black dick swung back and forth as he fought with Henrietta. She could see what she wanted, but couldn't get to it. It added strength to her struggle, so she was almost a match for the young boy. If he hadn't been country raised, she would have won, but he was large for his age, and above average in strength. George took pride in his strength, know-

by Donald Goines

ing that few boys his age could match him.

Slowly the old man crawled across the clearing,
dragging the vine with him. He finally reached
them. He helped to tie her hands, drawing strength
from his willpower, knowing the boy was lost
without his help. The two of them managed to tie
her feet so that she couldn't kick.

"The stick, the stick," the old man panted. "Get
it out of her," he said, before passing out.

George grabbed hold of the part of the stick still
sticking out of her, and began to remove it slowly.
A groan of pain escaped from the young, naked
woman as he slowly removed it. When it finally
came out, a rush of dark blood came out of her
wound and covered his hands. George twisted his
face away from the sight, but not too quick to
know that Henrietta had passed out from the pain.

George sat in the clearing holding the old man's
head in his lap. He didn't know what to do. He
couldn't carry both of them at once, and he didn't
want to leave either one behind. If he had to, he
knew that he would have to leave his sister. He still
couldn't get over the way she had carried on. One
thing was fixed in his mind. She hadn't recognized
him, her own brother. Whatever them crackers had
given her, it had messed her mind up. It hadn't
really come to him until then that what they had

given her was that strong. But now he knew that it had driven her insane. She was beyond recognizing either him or her grandfather.

The night passed slowly. Henrietta fell into a deep sleep, exhausted by the passions that had overtaken her. George kept the old man's head cradled tightly against his chest. Early in the morning old Ben's eyes fluttered open. He looked up to his grandson and began to speak in a hushed, weak voice.

"Ain't her fault, boy, yo' hear me? She don't know what she been doing. Remember the stick. Ain't no sane woman goin' do that to herself, boy, remember that." For a brief moment the old man's eyes held his, then the old man repeated the same words over and over, trying to make his grandson understand. "Ain't her fault, boy, 'member that always, ain't her fault." The old man tried the words again, but no sound came forth. He had died, using the last of his strength trying to explain to his young grandson that whatever his sister had done, she wasn't to be blamed.

Daybreak came and the birds sang in the trees while the squirrels danced along the high branches. It was a sight George often took enjoyment from watching, but this morning his heart was too sad to even notice.

"Grandpa." The sound of the voice shook George. It was a voice from the past. The voice of a little girl that he remembered so well. He turned his head and saw Henrietta crawling toward the dead body of their grandfather. He rose to his feet and cut the vines that had bound her feet. She said nothing to George but continued to crawl until she reached the old man. She held his stilled head in her lap and began talking to him.

It took a moment for George to become aware of it, but it finally dawned on him that Henrietta didn't know that the old man was dead. She was in a child-like state, and she couldn't tell the difference. She kept asking grandpa to get up, then asking George to wake him up. The child-like voice, her inability to recognize either of them the night before, and now her child's vision of death. It came to George that Henrietta was acting as she had when she was ten years old. Shocked and frightened, George walked over to the body and picked the old man up. As Henrietta watched him with a blank, almost idiotic expression, George hoisted the body upon his shoulder and began to stagger back toward the river. He kept one thing in mind, it would be much easier once he reached the river.

Henrietta followed along behind her younger

brother like a little girl, skipping and running. Never once did she offer to help. Once she came back and asked, "Grandpa sick?" Before George could think of a reply, she had forgotten she had even asked the question and ran off, chasing a butterfly.

As George watched his sister skip down the path, it occurred to him that she was as naked as the day she was born. The Henrietta he knew wouldn't have allowed him to see her in her bra, let alone stark naked. The more he thought of it, the angrier he became. His anger helped him to carry his burden. The rage he felt inside became so consuming that he ceased to notice the weight of the old man across his shoulders.

The sight of Henrietta, dancing naked, stripped of her pride and womanhood, fed fuel to his anger. He remembered his grandfather's last words, and they now carried meaning. Now that she was acting like a child he could see the real harm that had been done to her. Now he realized why they had been able to take advantage of her. Who couldn't take advantage of a ten-year-old child, he reasoned. Not knowing that much about the drug they had given her, he believed this was its effect. His anger was deep, a time bomb that was counting down until eventually it would have to explode.

The shattered little family reached the river and George put the body of his grandfather into the boat. He begged Henrietta to get into the small canoe, but she skipped up and down the river's edge, laughing and tossing small dirt clods at him. Finally, after he pretended to shove off without her, she came running down toward the water, crying like a child. The sight tore at him until he thought he would cry himself.

It was a slow trip home. Goerge was afraid Henrietta was going to tip them over, because she wouldn't remain still. Finally they reached the cabin. George got out and pulled the boat up onto the shore, then lifted up his grandfather and carried him onto dry land.

Henrietta screamed out in joy and ran toward the cabin. "At least she recognized that much," George said out loud, already talking to himself in the manner of men who spend a lot of time by themselves.

The ground was soft, so it didn't take George long to dig out the grave. He was going to bury his grandfather right next to where they had buried his father. The thought occurred to him as he dug that he would never be lucky enough to be buried beside his father and grandfather. There was no one to bury him. The feeling was powerful, he knew he'd never rest beside them.

George finished the digging, and now set about trying to make a coffin. His first problem was finding enough wood for the job. He considered taking some of the lumber from the old cabin at the water's edge, but then remembered some timber out behind the old cotton patch. It took some time to drag the wood back to the cabin where he could work and still keep his eyes on Henrietta.

George had already gotten into the habit of thinking of Henrietta as a child. He wondered if the drug would ever wear off and if she'd ever return to normal. But deep inside he knew that the damage had been done. She'd be this way until the day he buried her here beside her only kin. The thought that she might outlive him never entered his mind.

George slowly dressed his grandfather in his best clothes, an old cotton suit that the old man had bought thirty years ago. After dressing the body, he carried the old man out to the grave where he had left the coffin.

Never had anything hurt him as the happenings of the past twenty-four hours had. As he thought about revenge, he regarded the child-like girl standing beside the grave crying. The sight of the old man in the coffin must have triggered off something in her mind. As he pushed dirt onto the top of the coffin her crying turned to deep sobs, the sounds one hears only from the truly bereaved.

Henrietta was standing with her head down, crying her heart out. Tears began to roll down George's cheeks. He stood beside the grave and cried. Between tears he promised himself that one day there would be an accounting. The Jones brothers would pay for the crimes they had committed against his family, and they would pay with their only possession, their lives.

"Come on, child," George said softly, taking Henrietta's arm and leading her away from the grave. He could come back anytime and finish the job. Right now, he wanted to get Henrietta back to the cabin. Maybe once away from the grave, she would forget. He went over to the old truck, parked in front of the cabin and pulled out a small stuffed puppy. In a few minutes Henrietta was busy playing with the toy.

George sat down and began to think. It would be hell without the old man around, but they would make it. They had to. He got up and warmed some beans they'd had the night before on the stove. The old black stove was a relic of the past, with two burners on the top. But it was always kept clean and usable, like everything around the farm.

While the beans heated up, George slipped out and finished covering up the grave. He packed the dirt around the grave firmly, though he wasn't too worried about any animals coming around digging it up. As he worked, a greeting came from the direction of the river. He glanced up to see old Mr. Jefferson. With him was his sister's son, Little Bro, a huge Negro who was a hard worker but a slow thinker. The huge man's mind had been snapped when, at the age of fourteen, he had been beaten up by a bunch of white men in the woods. He had interrupted them while they were raping two young black girls from the plantation.

The sight of the men didn't make George happy at all. He hadn't had the time he needed to sit down and plan. The experience of seeing his sister raped, then his grandfather's death was too much. He needed to be by himself. It was too soon for any kind of company.

For a brief second, George thought of fleeing to the woods, even if he had been seen by the men. But the thought of Henrietta being left alone with them was troubling, even though the girl didn't have anything to fear from the men.

As they pulled their boat up out of the water,

George noticed that old man Jefferson had a suitcase in his right hand. Jefferson came on ahead of the younger man, leaving him to make sure the boat was secure.

"Howdy, George," the elderly bent-over man said as he puffed up the trail. It was easy to see that the short walk carrying the suitcase had worn him out. "I wouldn't have come out so late, but Little Bro stopped by, so I took the opportunity to have him row me out. Never know when 'nother chance like that would come, so I brought your sister's bag."

Jefferson stared down at the mound of earth. Then took off the old black hat he wore. "I started to come with the child, boy, but them honkies would have killed me sure as hell." The old man looked away. He looked pathetic standing there, self-consciously wanting to downgrade himself because he believed Henrietta had been killed.

George could see the baffled hurt in Jefferson's eyes, but didn't understand the reason for it. "It ain't my sister under the dirt, Mr. Jefferson," George said, watching the surprise, then the joy come into the man's face.

Suddenly the thought hit Jefferson that it couldn't be anyone else but his old friend. In the many years he had known the old-timer, he had never beached a boat without the old man coming out of the cabin and greeting him before he was on dry land.

A tear appeared in the corner of Jefferson's eyes as he looked around quickly. "It ain't the old man under there, is it?" he asked, hesitatingly.

"Uh-huh!" George looked away. He didn't want to see the hurt in Jefferson's face. Maybe the old man was realizing that his time was getting near. All his old pals were going on to that other world, and yet he lingered on.

"Howdy, Georgie boy," Little Bro called out as he came up the path, wiping sweat from his forehead with the ends of his shirt.

"How come you up here diggin', George?" Bro asked foolishly.

"Grandpa passed away this morning," George answered quietly, wanting to get the question and answer bit over with. He reached up and felt his temple. His head had started to hurt, he knew he needed to relax, to just sit down and do nothing for a while. But he wouldn't be allowed that luxury for some time yet. He would have to attend his guests just like Grandpa would have done. Now that he was the man of the house, he'd have to act like one.

"Well I'll be damned!" Little Bro cursed. "If

you all be needin' help out here Georgie, you just come on over to Mr. Wilson's place and let me know."

The question had to be asked, but Jefferson didn't want to ask it. He waited until they started walking up the path that led to the cabin. "George, what happened to him? I mean, did he just go asleep and pass over, or have one of them there strokes people be havin'?"

George hesitated for a second. It had to be said. They would see Henrietta in a minute anyway, and that would need explaining, so it was best to get it out and in the open.

"I don't know just what killed him," George began, "but I think it was the sight of what them honkies did to Henrietta that done it."

There it was again, and this time Jefferson couldn't dodge the guilt. The Jones boys had followed her out of town like he'd thought, yet he hadn't done anything. He could have gone to the sheriff or something, even though he doubted that it would have done any good. But then, at least, he might not have felt so responsible. If he'd done anything other than just go back into the bar and start sweeping the floor, he wouldn't have felt so guilty.

When they reached the cabin, George went in

first and the men followed. One look at Henrietta was enough. Jefferson blinked his eyes in shock. He couldn't believe what he saw. There was a child in front of him now, and not the little lady who had stepped off the bus the day before. The expression on Henrietta's face was that of a child. She sat on the wooden floor rocking her stuffed dog, singing softly in a child-like voice. When the men entered, she glanced up, then quickly went back to her toy.

"How long has she been like that?" Jefferson managed to ask, his voice shaking with emotion. "It don't seem possible that this is the same woman that got off the bus."

"She's been like that ever since me and gramps found her this morning in the woods. Ain't been no change since I brung her home. Been actin' just like a little girl, instead of a woman," George stated. The words were difficult to say, as if it hurt him to speak.

A sob escaped from Jefferson as he crossed the cabin floor and dropped down on his knees in front of her. "Miss Henrietta, gal, don't you 'member me, old Jefferson? You went and left your bags with me yesterday, child, don't you remember?" Tears rolled down the leathery cheeks of the man as he talked.

"You wanna play with my puppy?" Henrietta asked. "He's gone to the sleepy house now, sleepy house now," she repeated in a sing-song voice.

It was too much for old Jefferson. He moaned loudly, then jumped to his feet and fled. Little Bro stood dumbfounded as Jefferson ran past. He was undecided on what to do. Without someone to tell him what to do, and when to do it, he was at a loss.

"You better go now, Little Bro," George said softly. "The old man will be waiting for you to paddle him back home."

"I reckon I'll do just that, George, but don't forget now, if you all be needin' some help, just come yellin', boy, and Little Bro sure 'nuff will help you."

Need you, George thought as he looked away. I don't even know where to begin and the only help I get offered is from somebody in damn near worse shape than me. George walked out of the cabin and watched the man push the boat into the water. Little Bro raised his arm and waved, but Jefferson didn't even turn his head. As George watched the small boat grow smaller and smaller, he wondered why Mr. Jefferson had taken it so hard. It was as though Jefferson had seen what had gone on underneath the trees of the forest, but George knew the old man hadn't been there. Whatever the reason, he realized that he and Henrietta were going to need much more than pity. He figured he could take care of himself, but it was a new thing to him trying to take care of somebody else. It might be hard, George reasoned, but he'd make damn sure Henrietta never went hungry. He promised himself and his grandfather that he'd always look after his troubled sister.

7

THE ONLY BAR IN TOWN was crowded. Saturdays were generally good for business, but this weekend was extra busy. On top of that, old man Jefferson had been ailing for the past two weeks, leaving the fat, round-faced Tom Turner by himself to run the drugstore and the bar.

Ten men sat drinking in the small, homemade bar. Two tables, a long plank with stools in front and scattered chairs comprised the furnishings of Turner's crude little bar.

The sheriff stood with his back to the bar,

speaking harshly to the Jones brothers. "Now boys, I ain't got no complaint yet, but we all know what happened to that black gal." The sheriff, who was called Ed by most of the white men around, had heard the rumor the same as everybody else. The Jones boys couldn't help but brag, and Zeke had publicly displayed Henrietta's stocking earlier that week. Ed let his hand drop to the western Colt 45. "Now I don't particularly like blacks, but by the same token, I don't care for a lot of whites either." He waited, like an actor, poised, for the right moment. "But I did like that old nigger out there on the edge of the swamp." His voice lashed out at the men. It was cold and full of contempt. "Now I went out there lookin' and found the old man's grave and saw the gal. She can't talk, and the boy won't talk. But if ever the day comes," he was yelling now, something he rarely did, "that that gal gets her sense back and talks I'll hound you white crackers out of this swamp!"

The men inside the bar were silent now. Everybody had their eye on the aging, bent sheriff. There was nothing weak about the old man. He was still one of the best trackers around. He knew the swamps as well as any white man, and as good as some of the niggers.

The sheriff's old grizzly eyes, a pale yellowish

gray, bloodshot now from too much corn likker, pierced each Jones brother as he studied them closely. Each man felt fear as he stared at them. The sheriff was an old man who didn't take chances. He never brought a man out of the swamps alive.

Zeke, his dirty blond hair hanging down to the table top, leaned over his drink and said: "We don't know why you bad mouthin' us, sheriff, but I want you to know Ed, we don't know a fuckin' thing 'bout that ol' coon out there on the edge of the swamp." He picked up his glass and made a motion around the table toward his brothers. "We didn't know a darn thing was wrong with him." His brothers nodded their heads in agreement.

The sheriff stared right at them like he hadn't heard. "I'm goin' say it, and say it one time so you boys will know that I know what I'm talkin' 'bout. It ain't somethin' that been told me. 'Course a few people have done it too, but it's what I saw with my own eyes." His voice was slow and heavy, a warning that he was dead serious. "Them tracks out there was as plain as day. I even know who laid in the woods and watched what you boys were doing."

His words shook them. It was obvious as they glanced at each other. Zeke tried to laugh it off.

"Boys, looks like the ol' cuss done went back in them swamps once too often. Got swamp fever. Done seen it before, so I knows what I'm talkin' 'bout."

"Glad you have, Zeke, so if you ever see me comin' at you with my old shotgun," Ed stated, "you just write it off as swamp fever."

"Now Ed," Zeke continued, proud of the way people were leaning over to hear what he had to say, "you done told us what might rile you up, now I want you to know 'bout what might rile me. If one of my brothers was to come out of the back waters over on his belly 'cause of you and that ol' shotgun of yours, I'd think the fever done got the best of you and I'd have to treat you like a mad dog!"

Sheriff Ed studied the brothers. Zeke was doing the talking, but he wasn't the one the trouble would come from. Jake, the oldest, was sitting back in his chair and listening. That would be the one he'd have to kill first. With the brains gone, the rest of them would fall right in line—in line with the sight of his gun.

"I reckon we understand each other then," Ed said, as he pushed away from the bar, and walked slowly out the door. He had other things on his mind. He stopped on the porch and lit an old black cigar that was no longer than his thumb.

Them eyes had been the problem, Ed thought. That boy George had seen hell, and somewhere on the trip he had lost his soul. He had the eyes of a dead man, yet not dead. He had seen the look in a bobcat's eyes. The cat had somehow fallen out of her tree into the river, right into the midst of a group of alligators. The cat's eyes reflected the shock at first, then as the alligators encircled her and came straight at her, the eyes reflected the knowledge that she was about to die. Without hesitation, the cat had attacked the first alligator, dying with a complete disregard for her own life. Yeah, Ed said under his breath, that boy is sure going to be trouble one of these days. He's like one of them animals back there in the back waters. Moves like them too.

Ed opened the jail door and went inside the small office. He pulled the chair from behind the desk and opened the bottom drawer. He took out his personal jug of Red Eye, and drank from the flask. He sat down in the old wooden chair and remembered the day when he was way back in the swamp and had seen the boy. At first he had been surprised. There were few men who knew about that part of the swamp. To go back that far, you had to know your business, or you'd never find your way out. The boy had paddled by him that day going even deeper into the back waters.

The sheriff moved around nervously in his chair. He knew trouble was coming sooner or later. Rednecks like the Jones boys brought it with them wherever they went. And, it was just the beginning of the storm. The finish would be the darkness at the center. And yet, they hadn't even seen the dark, threatening clouds that were even now gathering on the horizon.

After the sheriff had left, Willie, a redneck handyman who did whatever kind of work he could get around the county, came over to the Jones brothers' table. "Zeke, ol' coon, you sure 'nuff let that old man know what size can to hang on his tail."

The compliment filled Zeke with pride. He grinned and glanced around at his brothers. "By God, I reckon we did let him know we ain't goin' take no houndin'."

Both of the younger boys broke out in loud laughter. Sonny-Boy let out a rebel yell. Turner, the bartender, acted as if he didn't hear them. He was afraid of all four of them. To him, they were like wild animals who had found their way out of the swamp. Violence was too close to the surface when you were near them. Turner feared physical violence worse than anything else in the world. Ever since his childhood days, he had feared men who were quick to punish with their fists.

Zeke, feeling his drinks, called out loudly, "Hey, Turner, how 'bout bring us a bottle of rotgut over here?"

Turner glanced up from where he had been serving drinks. The last thing in the world he wanted, was to give out more credit to the Jones family, but one look at the cold fish eyes of Jake was enough to make him change his mind. The bartender broke out another bottle of his cheapest whiskey and carried it over to the table.

"I hope you boys is keepin' count of how much you owe me for this stuff?" he said in his most submissive tone of voice.

"By God, we ain't never been troubled before 'bout us payin' off our debts," Zeke answered quickly, glad to get the extra bottle. He didn't bother to mention that Turner was the only person who allowed them credit.

Turner walked away from the table, then turned and came back. "I just want you boys to know, that's the last bottle you'll get out of me until you pay somethin' on that rear bill of yours."

The conversation in the bar dropped to a whisper, then picked up again after the other men saw that nothing else worthwhile would be said. Enough had passed back and forth tonight for most of the men to make their wives happy when they got home and reported all the latest gossip.

The bottle of whiskey didn't last long with all four of the Jones brothers and Willie drinking it as fast as they could raise their glasses. Zeke took the last swig. The other men watched as the last of their whiskey disappeared.

"You know," Jake said quietly, so that no one at the other tables could hear him, "it just might be time for us to pay that old gal a visit. I been wantin' to find out if she was still stump broke to my soft whistlin' anyway."

The men laughed, and Willie joined in even though he didn't know what was funny. "I sure would like me some of that black pussy," Willie stated, looking around at the others to see how his idea was received.

Zeke grinned. He had been waiting and wondering just how long it would take for Jake to make his mind up to pay her another visit. He had been ready himself, but was scared to go alone. "By God," he began, "all we'd need is 'nother ol' bottle of rotgut to carry 'long on the cold ride out there."

"Shit," Jamie stated, not wanting to be left out. "It would take one of them there miracles people be talkin' 'bout, to get us 'nother one of them bottles out of old Turner."

"By God, you ain't never told more truth than them words, Bro," Sonny-Boy piped in. "It would take thunder and lightnin' on a bright sunny day to make that tight-fisted ol' man give us 'nother jug to go along the road."

Jake stood up, and removed his rifle from under the table. "You boys walk over to the door, but don't go out. I'm goin' see if I can't make one of them, what y'all call miracles." Jake staggered over to the handmade bar, while the men shuffled slowly toward the front door.

Jake waited for Turner to come down to his end of the bar, then stuck his gun out and leveled the barrel at the old man's stomach. "We was thinkin' 'bout leavin'," Jake began slowly, "but the night air's kind of chilly. Now I been thinkin', next time I see one of them big bucks out in the woods, I just might knock him over and lug him in for you. That ways, you'll have fresh meat for some time to come."

"Well I thank you Jake, for thinkin' 'bout me like that. Could sure as hell use some of that meat you talkin' 'bout." Turner tried to ignore Jake, but the cold metal of the rifle convinced him to pay attention.

"Like I was sayin'," Jake continued, grinning dangerously, "it's chilly out there tonight, so me and the boys could use that other bottle." He kept the barrel in Turner's stomach. He could see the fear in the old man's eyes, and that did him more good than all the whiskey he had drunk. Jake always enjoyed the power he felt when he knew another person feared him. It was even more enjoyable when it was a white man because most of the time he had to find his joy amongst the blacks.

"Well now," Turner began, "I don't know if I can . . ."

"As I was sayin'," Jake interrupted, "I goin' bring you some fresh meat. Now you wouldn't be callin' me no kind of liar, would you, Turner?"

Turner made the mistake of glancing up into Jake's cold pale blue eyes. He trembled so much that other men watching could actually see him shaking in his boots. The bartender grabbed up the nearest bottle, a more expensive brand than he ordinarily gave them and offered it to Jake. "Here, Jake, take it. I'll be lookin' for that meat now," Turner said, trying to get back some of his self respect. "I don't generally buy a pig in a poke without seein' it, but good as you boys shoot, I ain't worried about it."

"Don't worry 'bout a thing," Jake replied as he

by Donald Goines

carried the bottle toward the door. "One thing the Jones boys is known for is keepin' their word."

The four men at the door watched Jake eagerly. As he approached, they slapped him on the back, offering congratulations and laughing loudly as they left the bar.

After their departure, there was a general sigh of relief. With the Jones brothers around, one never knew what form of entertainment might be in store. The brothers got their kicks by making other men crawl. It was the one area in which they lost their bigotry. It didn't make much difference whether it was a white man or a black man who was on his knees in front of one of their rifles—as long as he was down and crawling.

With Jake now in the lead, the men walked swiftly through the woods and to the river. There were five of them, so they took two boats. Jake sat in the center of his boat, sipping the whiskey he had "borrowed" from Turner. Willie and Zeke did the paddling.

"Save me a swallow of that there jug, Jake!" Zeke stated, unable to remain silent and wait until Jake finished his private drinking.

"Boy," Jake replied hotly, "if you get on my nerves, by God, I'll pour the rest of this crap in the river!"

Zeke didn't reply, he knew his brother too well. If the older man was riled, he'd do just what he said and dump all the whiskey into the water.

None of the others said anything, but watched anxiously as Jake took another long swallow from the bottle. Zeke licked his lips and looked away. He couldn't stand the sight of his brother hogging all the whiskey.

Finally, Jake motioned to Sonny-Boy to bring his boat closer. Jake held the bottle out to Sonny-Boy and grinned as he took it. He glanced back so that he could see the look of longing on Zeke's face.

"What you go and do that for, Jake?" Willie whimpered. "Them boys goin' drink it all!" He was downhearted.

"Them boys ain't crazy," Jake answered loud enough for the men in the other boat to hear. He wanted another drink himself. "Sonny-Boy," he called out, "you make damn sure you leave whiskey in there for all of us. These boys ain't even had a drink. I'ze just kiddin' a little with ol' Zeke. You know how he carries on over a snort."

Sonny-Boy laughed, took another long swig and wiped his mouth slowly. When he gave the bottle back, there was enough in it for everybody. Sonny-Boy laughed again when he saw the look of relief on his brothers' faces. He knew a man, even a brother, would have to be crazy to intentionally raise the anger of the Jones boys.

8

THE CABIN WAS QUIET EXCEPT for the soft singing of Henrietta. She had been humming the same tune over and over again for a week. George had heard her humming it so many times that when he didn't hear her light voice, he would glance up, and look to see what was wrong.

With the sun going down, the night noises rose from the swamp in a timeless chorus. The grunts of the bullfrogs and green frogs was continuous. It was a good sound because when they fell silent, a man started worrying. Silence meant that something alien was out there in the blackness. George listened to the noise, guessing at the different species of frogs. He heard the robber frogs, or barking frogs and visualized the short, squat, flat-headed amphibians. He chuckled to himself at the thought that they were no longer than two or three inches, but still able to make the sounds that sounded like a barking dog.

But as George listened, the sounds died. Everything became silent. He started to get up, and investigate but the frogs took up their noise again. Probably a passing bobcat, George told himself as he listened more intently now.

Five minutes later George heard a sharp whistle. The sound seemed to come from the edge of the wooded section of his land. George shivered as a cold chill climbed up his spine. He watched helplessly as Henrietta got up from the floor, dropping the toy puppy from her lap, and moving as if in a dream toward the door. Before George could pull himself together enough to stop her, she was gone. The whistle came again, and this time George realized what was happening. It came to him then that the Jones boys were on his land.

George's first impulse was to take his shotgun and rush down there amongst the trees and kill as many of the brothers as he could. But on second thought, he realized that if something happened to him, Henrietta would be left alone. Instead, he slipped out the back window and wormed his way into the woods.

George found the men standing in a circle as Henrietta approached them. They were grouped together in a small clearing near the river. They passed a bottle of whiskey back and forth in what seemed to George a dream-like pace. Henrietta walked into the circle and Zeke quickly took her dress off. She was like a small, unknowing child.

Tears rolled out of George's eyes as he watched. He did not know that this would be just the first time. In the next two years, George would climb out of the back window many times. In the nightmare black of those evenings, he would follow Henrietta to the same clearing and watch in anguish the rape of his sister.

Two long, helpless years and the young boy developed into a young man. The day finally came when George wasn't a boy any longer, but an avenging black man. He had gotten the size his youth had promised. Now, the coveralls he wore almost busted at the seams. His pants had to be rolled up around his knees. The shirt was too small, any attempt to button other than the two bottom buttons impossible. His black muscles bulged when he walked. During the past two years George had tried to cover up his hurt with work, and the fields showed it. Row upon row of well cared for greens, corn, and carrots. He had succeeded in keeping himself and Henrietta alive, surviving for only one purpose.

George had bided his time, waiting and planning. He never stopped hating the white crackers for what they had done. It was constantly on his mind. And now that spring was on them again, and the Jones came around at least once a week, his anger was growing even more intense.

One morning George watched as Henrietta became sick to her stomach. He was too naive to know what was wrong with her, so he waited. A month later he noticed the size of her small stomach. There was no doubt about it, she was going to have a baby. Never, the thought exploded inside his head. He would never allow Henrietta to have the white men's child.

For the first time the thought entered his mind to destroy Henrietta. It seemed to be the only choice he had. George was firm in his desire that she never give birth to the child, and that she'd be better off dead.

George started for the back window even before the sharp whistle. After two years he could tell from the whistle who it was. It wasn't the same ones all the time. Sometimes just the young ones would come over with a friend, other times just the two older brothers came. Lately, they had begun bringing other white men along for their outings in the swamp.

George remembered every new face. Each man was stamped on his mind like a picture. The only thing he believed would make the image of their faces go away would be their deaths.

Before leaving the cabin, George stopped and picked up his hunting knife and the old shotgun. As he climbed out the window, Henrietta started out the cabin door. She was walking like a zombie. It's all right, Sis, George said under his breath, it ain't many more of these nights in store for you, that I promise. The young man gripped his knife tightly as he moved silently through the rows of corn.

By the time George had made his way around the field and to the wooded section, Henrietta was already there. George's heart skipped a beat when he saw that there were only two of them. Young Jamie and Willie, the handy man, stood expectantly on either side of the quiet girl.

Neither of the two white men heard George crawling nearby. Ironically, Willie bgean to talk about him. "Jamie, ain't it strange we don't never see that ol' big buck she got for a brother?" Willie said. "I seen him in town at the store one day, boy. I'll tell you, that's one nigger I'd hate to run into out here."

"By God," Jamie replied, as he removed Henrietta's dress, "if you feel that way about it, what for you keepin' on comin' out here?"

Willie shook his head. "Well boy, you know how that is." He waited to see if Jamie was listening. The other man was busy placing Henrietta on the ground. She had to be moved into position. It was as if she was in a dream world all by herself.

"I don't mind comin' out here with you boys, Jamie," Willie said, "but you couldn't pay me hard cash to come out here by my lonesome. No sir," he said. They were the last words he was to ever speak.

The words were barely out of his mouth when George reached around the tree he was hiding behind and pulled the smaller man to him. His knife went in swiftly, while he covered the struggling man's mouth with his hand. Willie kicked, as George pulled the knife out of the man's back. He then brought it up in front to slit Willie's throat. Blood gushed out of the open wound, spattering across the clearing.

Jamie realized something was wrong when he felt himself being lifted up bodily from the young girl. "What the hell," Jamie cursed, being twisted around by George as if he were just a bundle of rags.

When he saw George's face, fear swept through his whole being. He vainly tried to bluff it. "By God, nigger, I don't know if you done went crazy or not, but don't no nigger put his hands on a white . . ."

That was as far as he got. His eyes came to rest on Willie's dead body. "My God, boy, you done killed a white man?" The shock at the sight was almost too much for him. Willie was slumped down against a tree, his eyes still open. "Don't hurt me, boy," Jamie begged, tears running out of his eyes. He didn't see any pity in the black man's face, but he didn't want to believe that a black man would have the nerve to really hurt him.

"Listen, boy," Jamie began, "Willie don't mean nothin'. I mean, if you let me go, I'll forget all about Willie comin' out here with me. You understand, boy, won't nothin' be said," Jamie tried to grin. "Why it'd be a joke between you and me. And, I promise, yes indeed I do," he continued, "we won't come around meddlin' that ol' gal, if that's what's got you riled."

George held him with one hand, shaking him like he would a mongrel dog. He didn't bother to speak, but just held him, staring deeply into the man's pale blue eyes. He saw Jamie's fear, but it didn't ease the tightly wound ball of hate inside him. When he heard Henrietta moan, George remembered his mission. He raised his knife and stabbed upward into Jamie's gut. When he pulled the knife out, half the man's intestines came with it. Blood spilled onto his hand, mixing with the blood that was already there.

As George worked the knife methodically into his victim, Jamie screamed like a wounded animal. The knife was everywhere he turned. He had never felt so much pain. It was as if the huge black man was trying to let him live, so that he could torture him even more.

It hadn't really been George's intention to get pleasure out of killing Jamie slowly. What was in his mind was what he had thought about over the past years, as he had watched them rape Henrietta. He had envisioned himself castrating each Jones boy, and that was what he was about to do. George slammed Jamie down onto his back, then grabbed him by his balls.

As Jamie realized what was happening, he began to struggle. He was so panicked that for a moment he got loose. But he had been stabbed so many times in the stomach that he couldn't have run ten feet without collapsing.

George flipped the wounded man onto his back. He bent over Jamie's bloody body and hacked off the man's penis and testicles. Jamie screamed and screamed again, until finally his voice began to fade out.

Henrietta sat on the back of her heels, watching her brother. She had no fear as long as George was around. He had fed her and washed her, and to her young mind he had taken the place of the mother she had never had. The screaming of the white man had bothered her, and she was glad when it had stopped.

George got up from where he knelt next to the dying boy. For some reason he didn't feel the joy he thought he'd experience once he had struck. Maybe it was because his job wasn't finished. Anyway, he decided as he rubbed his chin, these were two faces that wouldn't bother him during the nights any more. It dawned on him then that there wouldn't be too many nights left for sleeping. He'd have to move to the swamps now.

It was almost too dark for George to see in the small clearing, but he tried anyway. He kicked dirt over most of the large blood spots. Where Jamie lay was a large puddle of blood. George decided to come back early in the morning and cover up most of the messy spots.

After making Henrietta stay put, George began carrying the bodies down to the creek bed. He put both men in his large dugout, then went back for Henrietta. He decided that she would be all right if he left her alone. Once he got her in the cabin, she'd be okay. Because of the darkness, he knew she'd remain inside, unless one of them crackers came by and whistled for her. It would be a chance he'd have to take, because if he took her along for the ride into the swamps, anything could happen. It was dark, a snake might drop off a tree as they went under it. If not that, she might fall out while alligators were near. Without light, he'd have a time of it trying to look out for her. He remembered her bad habit of leaning out the boat whenever she rode, playing with the water or flowers that drifted by.

When George left her at the cabin, he made sure to pick up his flashlight. He wasn't foolish enough to try the swamps at night without any light. Not if he wanted to live. He hurried down to his boat, flashed the light around and then shoved off. Picking up his pole, he began to move down the bend of the river swiftly. He glanced at the two bodies, then back to his old shotgun. Now he had their guns, but the only gun worth anything was a pistol that George had taken off Jamie. The old double-barreled shotgun that Willie had owned was old and dirty. George wondered if it would even shoot.

After ten minutes of steady poling, George sighed with relief. He was now past the bend where he could have run into one of the Jones family. George hesitated, wanting desperately to paddle down to their shack and give them a surprise.

First things first, he cautioned himself. If I get rid of these bodies I got all night to creep around over that away, he said to himself.

As he reached the back water, George lost his way. When he cut on his light, he saw his mistake. He had been searching for a quicksand pit that he knew of, but he had taken the bend that led to the small sand bar that was used by most of the neighboring alligators.

As he pulled back on his pole, he heard a bull alligator roar. It sounded as if the creature was right under him. He cut on his flashlight and saw that there were four of them swimming near the dugout. In the daylight they wouldn't have come near the boat, but with the pitch blackness of the back swamps, they were ready. Night time was their time to seek out the unwary.

George smiled to himself. What better way to rid himself of some unwelcome company. He moved to the middle of the boat, making sure he didn't tilt it over. Slowly he raised Willie's body up and slipped it over the side. Immediately he rushed back to his pole, and began to move back out of the way. The water exploded with movement. The alligators were each tearing off a piece of the meat that had suddenly fallen into their midst. The sound of the large bodies splashing in the quiet waters warned George that now the waters would be crawling with man-eating reptiles.

George quickly went to the other body and slipped it over the side smoothly, so that it hardly made a ripple when it hit the water. Again he didn't waste any time. He back pedalled until he was sure he'd be out of the way of the thrashing 'gators. Next, he tossed the shotgun over. He removed the pistol from his waistband. It would be a waste to toss it over. Once the Joneses got the idea in their heads that it was him that had murdered their brother, whether or not he had their brother's gun wouldn't make any difference. He decided to keep the weapon.

It was still dark when he reached the fork on the river. It was too early to go home, if it was still possible for him to reach another Jones boy. George rolled over to the nearest point in the river where the two banks were the closest. It was possible, just possible, he realized, that he might catch one of the brothers coming home before daylight. If he had morning chores to do, he'd have to come from town and take care of them. There was just a chance, and a very good one that all the Joneses didn't stay home last night. Jamie had gone out, so it was possible that one of the brothers had gone with him. George made himself as comfortable as possible, and decided to wait in ambush through the night. If any cracker came his way, George planned to kill him. He rubbed the cold steel of his gun. The taste of revenge was sweet, but he hadn't tasted enough. His appetite was whetted, and now that he had killed, it seemed easy. It wasn't as hard as he had thought, he reflected, once you started killing honkies. It was something that could easily become a habit.

9

SONNY-BOY WALKED OUT of the small, clean cabin on the Wilson's farm. He stretched his arms over his head, and let his eyes roam across the grass and nearby huts. All of the cabins were dark and quiet, holding sleeping people who were trying to get the last few minutes out of the sleep they had coming. Soon the bell would ring, and it would be time for the black workers going to the fields to start their long day.

As Sonny-Boy started down the walk, he thought about where he was and what he had done. You never could tell, he reasoned. The nigger of the woman he had stayed with might be any-where. He might be waiting, trying to take his anger out on the white man who had just used his black woman all night.

A smile flashed across Sonny-Boy's face. That ol' Maybelle, he thought, now that was a piece of ass, not like that sorry fuck Jamie and Willie had gone after. Sonny was tired of Henrietta. The woman's eyes worried him. He remembered the bright woman they had first stopped. Now, when he saw Henrietta, all he could see was a shell of what she had once been. When the brothers made love to her, she just lay there like a board. It was as though she could no longer feel anything. Her emotions had been used up that night in the big clearing. Now there was nothing, and no matter what Zeke or Jake had tried, they couldn't bring life to her. Sonny-Boy wondered idly for the hundredth time why Henrietta came to their whistle. She was like a well-trained dog, and once she arrived, the wooden Indian part of her took over. Maybe that was the reason her young brother had never tried to bother them. He had probably peeked at them once, and seeing how cold she was, figured it wasn't worth the trouble. Yeah, Sonny agreed, it just wasn't worth the time or effort.

Sonny-Boy took the short path down to the river, then quickly pushed the small dugout into the water. He picked up the paddle and moved without a break. As he glanced up at the sky, he slowed down. It wasn't any use. Why bust his ass for nothing. If he continued to rush, he still wouldn't get to the farm until daybreak. It would be light and everybody on the damn place would be up before he got there.

As Sonny-Boy slowed down, the first rays of dawn broke over the swamp. The night sounds suddenly disappeared, and the animals that had been in hiding all night stuck their heads out and welcomed the coming of day.

George squatted down beside his dugout. The call of a wild turkey somewhere back in the swamp greeted the new day. This would be a good place to do some muddin', George reflected, as he saw large fish swimming back and forth near the muddy bank. Even as the light began to penetrate the gloomy swamp waters, George watched a pretty hoop snake slither through the mud. George watched the many-colored snake disappear into the swamp.

George raised up and kicked some mud off the bank and into the water. It looked as if he had wasted his time, nobody was coming down the river this morning. He walked slowly back to his boat. He'd have to be thankful for what he had gotten last night. Maybe with luck, another small group of them might come around that evening. Anyway, George reasoned, he had work waiting for him back at his cabin. He had to clean up the clearing, cover up some of the blood he was sure he had missed the night before.

George moved to his boat. He shoved off and poled on down the river. Soon he was at the bend, and turned down the fork. Ten minutes hadn't passed before Sonny-Boy came paddling slowly down the creek. He had found what was left in the corn likker jug, and was taking his good time about getting home. He'd already decided that his back bothered him too much today, just in case Jake was thinking about taking them out to the field to pick.

Zeke glanced toward the bend that led toward Henrietta's cabin. Jamie and Willie would be finished with the nigger gal by now, he reasoned. For a minute he was tempted to paddle over and get another piece. Hell, he might even be able to make her respond this early in the morning.

It was all idle daydreaming, though. Sonny-Boy didn't have the slightest desire for Henrietta. He felt sorry for his brother, and decided to tell Jamie about the wonderful lay he had found. Who knows, he might even break down and take Jamie along one night, just as long as Jake didn't find out which black gal they were humping. Once Jake got wind of it, it wouldn't be private stock any longer.

by Donald Goines

Then that nigger would really have something to be mad about—all the Jones brothers pounding his wife. Sonny-Boy laughed, it was a hell of a thing being black. But then the niggers didn't really mind. If he had left her a dollar or two, the old buck would have been happy. But once he found out Sonny had rode his woman all night for nothing, the nigger would carry on something awful.

The Jones' farm came into view. Sonny saw that Jamie and Willie's boat wasn't there, but that was normal for the brothers. They were all renowned for taking their pleasures during the nighttime hours.

At the same moment, George was realizing his mistake. He had left Jamie and Willie's boat right there for anybody to see. He cursed himself for being a dumb nigger, then hurried and found a tow rope. He got back in his dugout and this time paddled. Moving quickly, he held his breath as he made the turn which would expose him to any one on the river. His luck held and he quickly paddled toward the back waters. He followed the same path that led toward the alligator's stronghold. When he reached it, he noticed many of the creatures up on the banks sunning themselves. At his approach, they quickly slipped into the water and disappeared.

Using a small axe he quickly made holes in the bottom of the dugout. The small craft began to sink slowly. He paddled back the way he had come. It wouldn't take long for the boat to disappear into the muddy waters. But the craft sank only on one end, while the other stood up out of the water. The boat was actually on a small sand bar, that was only visible when the water was low in the swamps.

It was a long time before anyone came around asking about Jamie and Willie. But then, about a week later, the old sheriff came by asking questions. His hound dog face was unreadable as he walked along the land, searching through the bushes.

George held his breath while the sheriff, accompanied by the Jones brothers and two other men, walked around his land. If they found any blood back in the woods, anything could happen to him. The men searched in silence, every once in a while looking back at George with suspicious looks.

Actually, Jake, Zeke and Sonny-Boy weren't worried about their brother. They believed Jamie and Willie had gone down the river, possibly to the next town. Jamie had always talked about seeing some of the country, and Willie was known for his

by Donald Goines

ability to disappear, then show up a month later,
only to confess that he had been working for some
farmer in the next town.

To the remaining brothers, the search was just a
lark. In fact, they hadn't meant to bring it to the
sheriff's attention about Jamie being gone, but the
man had asked them about Jamie's whereabouts.
Only then, did the Joneses admit that their brother
had disappeared.

For a reason known only to the sheriff, he
hadn't been taken by surprise. When the brothers
had mentioned another town where the boys might
be found, the sheriff had only stared at them
closely. "Do you boys really think so?" he had
asked simply.

A simple enough question, but there was something else behind it. The brothers waited patiently
while the sheriff played detective.

When Sheriff Ed returned from the woods, he
noticed how close the black boy kept the shotgun
to him. The sheriff decided to wait until that night,
when he could come back without any fools along,
and arrest the boy. His old eyes had found what he
believed was blood. It could be animal blood, so he
wanted to wait until after he'd had a chance to
have it examined.

Now was the time, Sheriff Ed decided, to bring

his dumb followers to heel, to keep them in the dark. If the Jones boys half suspected that their young brothers had been done away with, trouble would break out. Sheriff Ed knew also that the sight of the dugout in the back swamps would arouse their anger.

The sheriff led the way back to the boats. The men walked down the path single file. The sheriff watched them as they got in the dugouts. No, they didn't suspect a thing. Death was riding on their bootheels, yet they weren't even aware of it.

For a while there, the young Negro had me fooled, Sheriff Ed reflected. Yes, after the boy waited so long to take action, Ed had decided that maybe he never would. But that was all over now, the rabbit had come from his cover, transformed into a killer wolf.

The men grew uneasy as the sheriff led them deeper and deeper into the swamp. Jake Jones stared at him coldly with his dirty yellowish blue eyes. They seemed to glow like wild amber. Whenever he caught one of the other men glancing at him, he'd grin, revealing gaps amongst his yellow teeth.

Finally, Jake spoke, his voice raspy and soft. "Sheriff ain't takin' us way in the back waters for nothin', boys. He done got somethin' on his mind that he ain't tellin' us boys 'bout."

The sheriff, riding in the first canoe with one of his deputies, ignored Jake's remark. He was busy trying to figure out what had happened out here in the wild country. Once the other men saw the dugout he was leading them to, he was sure he'd have some angry hillbillies on his hands.

Jake resented the old man's attempt to ignore him. It was becoming clear to him that something had happened to Jamie, but just what it was he couldn't be sure of. After another attempt to draw the sheriff out, Jake gave up. He scowled angrily at his two brothers, as they poled their dugout slowly in the rear. Jake, paddling in harness with the other deputy, kept up with the sheriff, but his brothers had a tendency to drop far in the rear of the other two boats as they rowed weakly.

The two men the sheriff had brought from town, Jericho Canaan and his young brother Jitty, were both considered to be expert hunters and guides. The brothers earned their living from taking parties of big city men into the swamps to hunt. When they weren't doing this, they made money by filling in as deputies. Both men were dark-complexioned, with jet black hair that hung down around their shoulders. People in town called them red niggers behind their backs, but never to their faces. Before their mother had passed away, the Indian strain had been more evident. She had been part Seminole. A passing Irishman had romped in the grass with a Seminole squaw, and from that union the tree of Canaan brothers had been started. Other men shied away from them, their hawk-like features didn't attract company, nor did they seek the company of others. Neither man had taken a wife, yet they seemed content with each other. Their small cabin was west of town, located in a wooded section rather than in the swamps.

The banks began to get narrow, soon there was less than twenty feet separating one bank from the other. The branches of the trees overlapped. Hanging out over the murky water, the tree limbs offered continuous danger. The men used extreme caution as they silently poled their slim crafts through the water.

"Damn!" The word shattered the silence. It had seemed as if they were in another world. The sound of Sonny-Boy cursing broke the spell that had fallen on the small group of men.

Without warning a large alligator, disturbed by their passing, jumped from a sandy bank that he had been sunning himself on. He made a loud splash as he hit the water. The men looked quickly in his direction, but there was nothing to be seen.

The alligator was gone. The continual hunting of
them had made them overly cautious.

"Goddamn," Zeke said. "Did you see the size of
that bastard? He must have been ten feet long!"

"Ten feet my ass," the deputy in the boat with
Jake stated sharply. "Shit, boy, it's been years
since a ten footer been seen. They used to be
common back here in the swamps, but now'days
you'd have to go deeper in the swamps than we are
now before findin' one that big."

The men once again fell silent, each one watching the vines overhead. They were in close now,
and the snakes were an ever present danger.

Finally the sheriff rowed in to the bank. The
men in the two rear boats followed suit. The men
got out and stretched their legs. The sheriff led the
way up the moss covered bank. He walked only a
few feet, then stopped.

The canoe was laying up on firm ground where
the sheriff had dragged it from the creek to the
higher ground. The men filed around the boat,
each staring at it as though they had never seen a
dugout before. Finally Jake broke the silence.

"Well, Sheriff Ed, I reckon it's time you told us
somethin'. Seems to me you know somethin' we
damn well ought to be knowin'." Jake glanced
around at his brothers, then continued. "We all

know that's the fuckin' boat Jamie and Willie was in, now we'd like to know where the hell our brother is?"

"If'en you knowed their dugout was way back in here, Ed," Sonny-Boy asked, "why the hell was we lookin' around that coon's farm?"

Zeke, who was much slower than the rest of the men, finally figured it out for himself. "By God, Ed," he yelled at the sheriff, "you don't reckon that coon done did somethin' to Jamie, do you?"

The three brothers looked at each other. They didn't want to believe what their eyes were telling them. Had it been any one but their brother, they would have quickly marked him up as a goner. Finding the boat back in the swamps was enough evidence for just about anyone. Without a boat, no one could have gotten through the swamps, not as deeply as they had come.

"Just where the hell did you find that boat?" Jake inquired, his eyes blazing with an inner fire.

For the first time since landing, the sheriff spoke. "I reckon you boys might as well know," he began, "since you ain't goin' give me no kind of peace 'til I tell you." He rubbed his lean jaw, then continued. "You know where this creek twists around and comes to the bend a little farther back?" he asked, waiting for a reply.

Jake spoke up, all the smartness gone from his voice. His face had turned a grayish hue, all the color drained from it. "You ain't talkin' 'bout that bend where all them 'gators be at, is you, Ed?"

Death was always like this, the sheriff reasoned. Men never wanted to face it when it struck close to home. "That's the place, Jake. I come around the bend and found their dugout overturned right there." He stopped, waiting for his words to reach them. "Now, I don't know if them boys was back here huntin' 'gators or not, but that's where their dugout was overturned."

"Goddamn almighty," Zeke cursed loudly. "Wasn't nothin' back there but the boat? I mean, you couldn't find no bodies, or nothin' like that to prove they was dead, did you?"

The sheriff hesitated, not wanting to answer, then changed his mind. "Zeke, maybe you don't know what's around that bend, but your brother Jake sure in the hell does. It's enough 'gators to eat up everything in the swamps includin' us and not leave any sign. It's where they breed at, and God have mercy on anybody who overturns a canoe back in there."

"Shit!" Sonny-Boy said. "Everybody here is a swamp man, Ed, so we don't need no bullshit. Now, if it was city people, that would be somethin' different, but we all know a 'gator ain't goin' bother no man, so ain't no reason to make us think them boys done got ate up by 'gators."

The sheriff looked at him as if he had lost his mind. "Boy, I don't know where you got that shit at, but I'll tell you this much. Maybe one 'gator won't bother no man, but when you get a whole pond of them together, they'll eat any goddamn thing they can get their teeth in. Now, if them boys was drinkin' and made the mistake of gettin' their boat turned over back in there, them 'gators would have got to them before they could swim to the bank. Now you ain't got to take my word for it, just ask your brother, Jake. He'll tell you if I'm lying or not."

Both boys glanced quickly at their older brother, though neither one really needed Jake to say anything. Each man knew how dangerous an alligator was. True, they would run at a man's approach, but when the water was full of them, they were very unpredictable.

"It don't make no difference about them 'gators, noway," Jake began, " 'cause Jamie wasn't 'bout to come back in here at night huntin' none. No sir, not on your life. If it was anybody but Jamie, I might have gone along with it, but that boy was too scared of the swamps at night." Jake glanced around, making sure his words were understood. "So I reckon our best bet is to get back to that black nigger's place and maybe with a little rope we can get the truth out of him." He didn't wait to see if anybody was following. He started walking back toward the boat. As far as Jake was concerned, it was cut and dry. Somebody had brought Jamie back into the swamp against his will.

Zeke caught up with Jake, asking questions of things he couldn't figure out himself. He couldn't believe something had really happend to Jamie. He'd have to see more then he'd seen so far before he'd believe his brother was dead.

As they reached the dugouts, Jake leaned over to push his boat down the bank. The shotgun blast passed over him and caught Zeke in the stomach. Zeke let out a scream and pitched over on his back, clutching at his guts. Another roar from the shotgun, and this time the shot caught the young deputy, Jitty, in the face as he came running out of the bushes to help Zeke.

"Get down, get down," Sheriff Ed yelled at his men.

Deputy Jericho ignored the warning as he ran to his brother's aid. He picked the young man up and held him in his arms. Tears ran down his cheeks as he realized that his brother would never speak to him again. He mopped the blood out of his brother's eyes, but it wasn't any use. The shotgun blast had torn away most of Jitty's upper face.

The sight of Jitty made Sonny-Boy want to puke, but the fact that his own brother was also down drove the thought from his mind. Jake had his rifle to his shoulder as he searched the opposite bank for movement, but he saw nothing.

With the help of the sheriff, Sonny-Boy dragged Zeke's body back out of range of the shotgun. With the rifle still held ready, Jake walked backwards away from the narrow creek, scanning the trees and bushes of the opposite bank for the source of the danger.

Sheriff Ed glanced down from his cover at his deputy who still was beside his young brother's body. If Jericho didn't get himself killed, Sheriff Ed reflected, he'd never be the same man. The death of his kid brother would drive him crazy.

The cries of the wounded man came to him. He'd already examined the wound, so Ed knew Zeke didn't have long to live. By the time they got him out of the swamp he'd be dead. Zeke had taken most of the buckshot in the stomach, so it was just a matter of time. For one of the few times in his life, the sheriff wished that a man would hurry up and die. If Zeke would pass on, then they could get right on the bushwacker's trail without losing any time. But if they had to go back to town, then they would just give the killer that much time to set up another ambush.

"What we goin' do, sheriff?" Sonny-Boy screamed hysterically. "My brother's dying, sheriff, he needs help!"

Sheriff Ed glanced back at the frantic young man. "Just take it easy, son," he cautioned. "We goin' get him out of here. I just don't want any more of you to get hit, that's all." As he watched Sonny-Boy, Sheriff Ed realized that the brother wouldn't be any help in tracking down the killer. He counted on who he could use. Jericho would be a lot of help once he got over the shock of his brother getting killed. Yes, with Jericho and Jake helping him, he'd flush George out of his hole. He rubbed his chin slowly as he thought it out. There was no doubt in his mind about who the bush-wacker was. The only problem lay in catching up with the young black man before he killed again.

10

AS SOON AS THE SHERIFF and his men left, George went into action. He had read the warning in the sheriff's eyes. "I'll be back," they had said—it was as plain as day. The only problem was that George wasn't planning on waiting for the old sheriff to come back and arrest him.

George went into the cabin and quickly packed everything he thought he and Henrietta might need. He took all the sugar and salt in the house, plus whatever toys he could find for Henrietta. Meanwhile, she sat against the wall playing with her toy puppy, staring at him with large, uncomprehending eyes. Having packed everything into Henrietta's two suitcases, he carried them down to the river and put them in the large dugout. After three trips he was ready. George then led his sister out of the cabin, pulling her along by her hand. He had taken the time to dress her in a smart pants outfit he had found amongst her clothes. He'd then made her put on her high boots, figuring that it was the best protection he could give her against snake bite. He knew it wasn't much, but it would have to do.

George sat Henrietta down amongst the boxes and suitcases, then put his oars down into the bottom of the boat and used his pole to push off. The oars would come in handy eventually, but most of the time he'd need the pole.

Leaving the farm, he poled swiftly away from the only home he'd ever known. As he reached open water, his eyes went to the shotgun laying at his feet. He wished he'd been able to get the rifle that Jake Jones had taken from his father, instead of the pistol he had taken from Jamie Jones. But it would have to do, until he was able to ambush Jake and get the rifle that rightfully belonged to him.

George figured that the sheriff and his men had gone deep into the swamps. If he hurried, he might be able to catch them while they were still in deep and even up the odds. With that thought in mind, he poled the dugout even faster. Every now and then, he'd glance up to make sure Henrietta was staying quiet.

George watched Henrietta closely. He had warned her about letting her hand fall into the water. But as soon as he'd look away, she'd quickly put her hand back into the water and let it stay there. Whenever he'd look up from his poling and see her doing it, he'd search the water quickly, looking for any sign of water moccasin. The four-foot water snake was extremely dangerous. Heavy and dark, the lethal swamp snake would strike without warning. Just the sight of Henrietta's hand dragging along in the water was enough to make one of them attack.

George gave his sister another warning as he came to the bend that would lead them into the back waters. Now he poled slower as he searched for signs of the sheriff and his party. The last thing he wanted was to come face to face with the group. When he reached the turn that led back to the 'gator pool where he'd left the dugout, he passed it by. Farther down he took another twisting turn and followed it until the banks began closing in on them. Now he watched his sister closely, knowing that the danger was ten-fold. He searched the swinging vines, hoping that he could see danger before it struck out at them.

Suddenly they came to a spot that appeared to be land but wasn't. The water was covered with moss. Every now and then an old tree stump could be seen. As George poled, he saw something coming through the moss covered water. He warned Henrietta, not knowing the exact nature of the approaching danger.

As Henrietta removed her hand from the water, George let out a sigh of relief. His eyes still followed the movement, until he could make out a snake. From the short distance, he couldn't tell what kind it was, but most water snakes were dangerous, so it was best not to take any chances.

"Don't Henrietta," George ordered, sharply. She had begun to put her hand back in the water. With the moss covering the water, it was an exceptionally dangerous thing to do. He knew there was no way for him to make her understand, so finally he made her get up and come over and sit between his legs.

George followed the ageless trees through the dense swamp, picking his directions from them. Few white men knew about his destination. His father had brought him out here long ago, showing him how to tell from the old trees where he was. It was a hiding place his father and grandfather had both used before. Now it was George's turn to seek out the swamps for protection.

Finally George was past the stagnant water. He came to a small creek with fresh running water. Again the banks were close on both sides, but the stench of stagnation that had been so strong before was now gone. The willow trees seemed to beckon them, their branches swaying with the light breeze that came from the west.

The sounds of the swamp became intense as they went deeper and deeper into the wild marshlands. Alligators could be seen sunning themselves on the nearby sand bars. The deeper they went, the larger the alligators became. The huge reptiles looked up at the passing boat, then continued their sunning. Another small turn in the creek brought George into clear view of another breeding pond of alligators. They seemed to be everywhere.

Henrietta stared at the large creatures with fear-ridden eyes. As one of the huge reptiles came swimming past, her eyes opened wide in horror. They were everywhere. The banks were loaded with them, and they drifted slowly past in the water. The girl stared at them open-mouthed. George didn't have to worry about her putting her hand back into the water this time. Henrietta sat upright, clutching her toy puppy to her small chest as if she were frightened for the stuffed animal's life.

George continued to pole his dugout, only now, he had to move with a certain amount of caution. One mistake and it could be their last. As they moved down one of the pathways that led from the breeding pond, George raised his pole and swung it over Henrietta's head. Before she realized what had happened, George knocked a vine snake from its perch and into the water. The snake falling into the water lured two alligators from their sunning spots.

George watched the two long alligators as they moved quickly on their weak legs toward the water. Once in the water they moved smoothly, swimming with a gliding motion. "You won't find no dinner there," George shouted, his voice carrying into the wooded section of the swamps. Birds took to the wing because of the strange sound. The grunts of a wild pig could be heard, disturbed from its rambles also by the sound.

George continued to pole until he reached an old tree that was bent from age and leaning out over the water. He pulled in beside it, jumping out and pulling the dugout up out of the water. He took Henrietta's hand and led her ashore, instructing her to wait after making sure no vipers were near. Then he went back and got two of the bundles out of the dugout. He led the way up the small path. They walked for ten minutes, then came to a man-made clearing. Corn was growing wildly in neglected rows. Farther into the clearing was a small, crude cabin. With Henrietta following, George led the way toward the shelter. Once he got her settled down inside, he went back to the dugout and brought back the rest of the suitcases.

When he returned, his sister was still sitting where he had left her. He moved around the cabin quickly, wanting to get back to the water as quick as possible. When he finished, he instructed Henrietta to remain inside the cabin until his return. He wasn't sure she understood what he meant, but prayed that if she went out, she wouldn't walk too far into the swamp. There was a lot of quicksand around, and she wouldn't know how to tell it from the rest of the wet ground she'd have to walk on if she ventured out.

For a minute, George debated on whether or not he should put something against the cabin door so that she couldn't get out, but changed his mind. If something happened to him, she'd starve to death. She'd die anyway, he reasoned, if something did happen, but the swamps wouldn't be as cruel as starving to death would. Out in the swamps she'd die swiftly, without a lot of pain. Starving, would take days. The quicksand would only take a few minutes.

George pushed the dugout back into the water, picked up his paddles and began to row. It was faster, yet more dangerous, because he couldn't watch the hanging vines for snakes. But what he had in mind would necessitate speed. He wanted to reach the white men before they came out of the swamps. If he could kill the rest of the Jones brothers, his work would be finished. As he rowed, he remembered the sheriff and realized that whatever happened, he'd have to kill the old man too.

There was activity ahead of him as George neared the alligator pond. He could hear the loud splashing, as if something or someone was trying to get away. He slowed down and moved with caution, though he didn't believe the sheriff and his party had found their way down this pathway. The water would make them lose any trail they were following. As he neared the breeding spot, the noise became louder. As soon as he turned the bend he saw what the commotion was all about. A small doe had came down to drink, and stepped too near one of the logs which was drifting by. The object had suddenly come to life, catching the doe's front foot in its blunt snout. As the doe

fought wildly to break free, the alligator steadily
pulled the young animal deeper into the water.

The noise of the struggling creatures drew other
alligators to the scene until the doe was completely
surrounded. As George watched, the doe was taken
under water. A slight shiver went down his spine as
he passed them. The struggle had brought swarms
of alligators into the water. George put down the
paddles and picked up his pole. He expertly pushed
off of one alligator that got too near with his pole.

George wiped the sweat off his brow as he left
the pond behind. For one of the few times in his
life, the stagnant water didn't repel him. He went
through it quickly, watching for snakes which were
the only danger he had to worry about in this part
of the swamp.

Once out of the stagnant water, George picked
up the oars and began to row. He glanced up at the
sky, praying that the sheriff's party was still deep
in the swamp searching for Jamie. He knew without a doubt where they were. He had found the
sheriff's footprints, and followed them until he had
found the dugout the sheriff had pulled out of the
water. It hadn't taken much for him to see that the
sheriff knew about Jamie and Willie.

George smiled as he thought about the old man.
He had kind of liked the sheriff, ever since the old

man had begun to stop by the cabin and visit his grandfather. But like him or not, the old man would have to die. He knew the swamps too well. George had followed him too many times back into the marshland, surprised that the sheriff had known the old trails. It was rare indeed for a white man to really know the old trails, but the sheriff was one of those rare men.

Before George pulled in and hit his boat, he heard the voices of the white men. Sound carried far in the back waters. He had been listening for them, figuring that whites seldom moved along together without making some kind of noise.

After making sure his boat wouldn't be hard to get back into the water, George took his shotgun and crept down the bank. He sought out just the right spot to lay his ambush. With luck, he might be able to get three or four of them.

He found an old tree right across from where the party had left their dugouts. Laying the barrel of the shotgun across one of the lower branches, he took aim. The gun was sitting right in the crook of the fork, so that it wouldn't waver one way or the other. It was a perfect armrest. As he waited, George prayed that he would be lucky enough to knock off at least both of the older Jones brothers. Once he got them, Sonny-Boy wouldn't be much trouble running down.

Before George could grow tired of waiting, the men came from behind the trees. Zeke was arguing over his shoulder at Jake. Both men seemed to be side by side. For a moment George wondered if both barrels would bring them down. Then the fear of missing such a good opportunity made him change his mind. He took dead aim at Jake, wanting to get the oldest brother first.

At the same moment George squeezed the trigger, Jake bent down. George cursed under his breath as the sound of the shotgun exploded in his ear. He knew without even looking that he had missed. He quickly reaimed the weapon, but he couldn't get a clear shot at Jake. The man was hiding behind the boat. Then he saw Zeke, doubled over and clutching his stomach. At least he had hit one of the brothers. George wondered if a shot through the boat would reach Jake. If he only had the rifle the hillbilly had taken from his father. With that shotgun he could have fired through the boat and knocked off Jake without the least worry.

Suddenly, one of the deputies came running down the bank. Without a second thought, George raised the shotgun and cut loose at the man. He saw the buckshot strike the deputy in the face.

Even as the man fell, George knew he was dead. He cursed under his breath. Now, he had killed a man he hadn't even wanted to kill. But, he reasoned, if the sheriff planned on hunting him out in the swamps, he'd have to kill many more of the sheriff's deputies before they got the message.

George took his time and reloaded. The men were on their guard now, so he'd have to wait for another chance to hit them. It would come, if he was patient enough. Moving slowly, George backed away from the tree, keeping his eyes on the movement of the men on the opposite river bank. He walked quickly back to where he had left his boat. In another second, he was on the water and poling silently away from the sheriff and his small group of helpers.

11

AS THE AFTERNOON PROGRESSED, Henrietta grew restless. She knew her brother had told her to stay inside, but the cabin was hot. She removed the top of her dark brown pants outfit. With just her brown pants and white blouse on, she walked to the cabin door and peeped out. The sound of birds singing in the nearby trees reminded her of home.

Growing tired of the inside of the small cabin, she pushed the front door open. As the door opened, she fled to the rear of the cabin. She peeped out between her hands, and saw the door wide open. After ten minutes, she built up the nerve to walk back to the door. After peeping outside, she convinced herself that nothing was wrong with just stepping out.

The same moment that George pushed his boat down the small incline back into the water, Henrietta took her first step outside. It was a timid step, but when nothing happened, she built up her nerve and went even farther. She began to play in front of the cabin, then went back inside and got her stuffed puppy. She brought the toy outside and sat down in the dirt. The sun was hot on her bare arms, but she didn't mind the heat at all. Every now and then she'd glance up, hoping that she'd see George before he caught her disobeying him. As the time sped past, she forgot her brother's orders and began to move farther and farther away from the old cabin.

The sight of some wild turkeys drew Henrietta away from the cabin. She ran after the pretty colored birds, screaming loudly with joy. Her eyes were bright with happiness as she ran laughing after them.

Henrietta's screams of joy only frightened the birds, and they fled in panic, with the child-like girl in hot pursuit. The paths she followed were old and covered with weeds. By the time the birds were gone from sight, she was lost. For the next twenty minutes, Henrietta stumbled around the

by Donald Goines

small island with the luck of an angel.

At one time she was less than ten feet from quicksand, but the sound of a squirrel in the trees caused her to change her rambling direction. She caught sight of the bushy-tailed animal out of the corner of her eye and wandered toward it.

"Here puppy, puppy," she begged. "Please wait, please wait for me. I won't hurt you." When the small frightened animal disappeared, Henrietta sat down in the tall weeds and cried. She leaned against an old swamp tree that had seen better days. With her back against the tree, she tried to figure out why she had been crying. It was impossible for her to remember. She rested her head in her hands for one of her headaches had begun. She could feel the pain over her eye, and knew that soon her entire head would be throbbing with pain.

At times like this, Henrietta could almost remember certain things. The picture of a huge house came to mind. She remembered the pretty grass. There were many black people there besides George. When she thought of these things, her head hurt even more. But there was something that kept pushing inside her to come to life. One of these days, she hoped, she would be able to understand just what it was that kept bothering her.

Leaning back more against the tree, Henrietta

glanced up at the sky. Suddenly her heart froze, and she could hardly breathe. Her eyes grew large with fear, the whites showing wildly.

What she was watching would make many grown men shake with fear. She watched as the long snake wound itself along the tree branch.

If her brother had been there, he would have laughed at her, then taken his time and pointed out certain things about the snake to her. It was a common hog-nosed snake, unique, and at times amusing. When molested it hissed, spread, and struck as though to do harm, but it never bit. If the threats fail, it rolled over and played dead. Without giving the girl under the tree another look, the snake changed its direction and went on through the branches, searching for another way down. As long as she stayed there, he would never try to come down that way.

Finally Henrietta found the strength to get up and flee. As she ran south, she passed right on the edge of the swamp quicksand. The pretty flowers floated on top of the slow death, ready to be the headstone for the few unwary souls that chanced that way.

Meanwhile, George poled slowly away from the river bank. He was concerned with his next ambush. The men he left behind would be too busy worrying about whether or not he was still there to give any kind of chase. His smile of satisfaction quickly disappeared as he remembered that he had missed Jake. At least I got Zeke, he coldly reflected as he began to plot his next move.

George realized that the sheriff and his men would be watching every twist of the river, but he also believed he would be able to ambush them again without them realizing that he was near. The real problem was the boat. He had to be able to reach his boat after the ambush. He'd have to put it out of sight, most likely drag it up into the woods. If he did that, he'd still have the same problem of pushing it back to the water, and he might not have the time. They'd be out for blood, and right on his trail. For now, though, he had them. They hadn't expected it, but next time the sheriff would know it was to be to the death.

The sheriff had probably realized that George didn't plan on letting any of them get out of the swamps alive. With all of them dead, there would be no one to come after him, and then he would be able to return to his home. The thought of home made George think of his sister, and he began to worry. He prayed that she would be all right. If she would just stay inside the cabin for twenty-four hours, he just might be able to pull it off.

The more George thought about Henrietta, the more he realized she wouldn't be able to make it back in the swamps where he'd left her. No, she'd need constant watching, or something would certainly happen to her. As he thought about it, the desire to leave and hurry home became strong. He felt guilty for even thinking about her death. If he hadn't harbored such thoughts, he wouldn't worry so much. Now, if something happened to her, it would always be in his mind, and that he could live without.

As he thought about his sister, he caught himself poling the boat faster, so he brought his thoughts under control. To leave now and return to her would ruin everything. He'd end up missing the sheriff, and once out of the swamps, it would be only a matter of time before the sheriff told someone about him. It would be the end for him and Henrietta, because after that, even if he killed the sheriff, there would be others coming for him. Henrietta would never have a chance to go back to their farm. She'd have to stay in the back waters, and that would be the end for her. No, George reasoned, he had to stay. He laid the pole down and drifted as he brought his thoughts back to the problem at hand.

Wherever the ambush was, George would have to

be able to reach his boat. He couldn't allow the
sheriff's men to trap him on one of the small
islands. George closed his eyes and pictured all the
islands around, trying to remember the one that he
could cross with his boat. If he had the smaller
boat, it wouldn't be so difficult, but he had
brought the large dugout. For a moment George
debated on rushing back to his home and tying one
of the smaller boats to the rear of the large dugout.
No, he reasoned, it was too dangerous. They might
catch him in the open water. With their long-range
rifles they'd cut him to pieces before he ever got
close enough to cut loose with his old shotgun.

Thunder cracked far away in the eastern sky.
George glanced up at the threatening clouds. Some
time that evening, he figured, the storm would
reach him. Maybe with luck he'd be finished out
here, and could get to the clearing and fix dinner
for Henrietta.

At the moment the thunder roared, Henrietta
wasn't wishing for George, she was screaming for
him. Her tiny voice shattered the silence of the
back waters. Without warning, the brush in front
of her burst open and a young wild boar ran out.
The razorback had been startled from his lair by
her constant screaming. He came out angry and
snorting loudly.

The sight of the pig froze her in her tracks. She screamed over and over again. The high shrill sound seemed to frighten the boar. As he stood there almost hypnotized by her screaming, Henrietta came loose and began to run. Her young legs pumped up and down. She didn't run like a child. Her movements were those of a young woman who was accustomed to running.

Henrietta flew down the trail, not knowing where she ran, running blind. Branches and small hanging vines lashed her face viciously. All at once she found herself sprawled out on the ground, tripped up by an old tree root that was blocking the small path.

In her blind panic, Henrietta started crawling. The base of a large tree brought her up short. She began to crawl around it. The large roots at the base were huge and covered with moss. Tears ran down her cheeks. Her pants suit was ruined, it was covered with dirt and in her tumbling falls, she had managed to snag the pants in the right knee. The rip was widened by her frantic crawling.

Thunder sounded again as the storm neared. The cracking roar terrified her. Paying no heed to where she put her hands, she crawled over an exceptionally large root. The moment her hand came down in the soft moss between the roots, pain exploded in her arm. As she drew it back, she saw that her forearm was covered with small vipers, the deadly offspring of the cottonmouth snake.

The tiny pit vipers were less than two months old, but as poisonous as most grown snakes. Their nest had been disturbed and now they reacted like angry bees. Each baby snake was only about a foot long, not having reached the heavy build they would possess once they became full grown cotton-mouthes.

As Henrietta struck two of the small snakes from her arm, another one crawled over the root and struck her on the leg. Instead of getting up and running, Henrietta sat against the tree, wasting precious minutes fighting the tiny reptiles off, but there were too many of them for her. The nest had held over fifteen snakes, and now they were all aroused.

Henrietta finally managed to shake the snakes loose from her arm. She jumped to her feet, and for a moment dizziness overcame her and she rocked on her feet. As she glanced down, all she could see were dark wiggling forms around her. In the next second she was soaring over them. The quick jump landed her five feet away from the nearest cottonmouth, but the damage had been done. A scream burst from her lips as she began to run wildly.

The venom she had taken into her system didn't have time to take effect. Her wild aimless running took her straight down the path that led to the quicksand. From the power of her leg muscles, she was into the quicksand and deep into the middle of the pond before the mud brought her up short. When she couldn't move her legs any more, she stared around wild-eyed, unaware of what was happening to her.

The pull of the quicksand made Henrietta realize that she was sinking and she screamed at the top of her voice for George. Henrietta started to struggle as she sank deeper. By the time her waist was covered, the poison began to take its effect and her head drooped onto her chest. Henrietta passed into unconsciousness before the ooze was able to claim her.

The sounds of the swamp came alive again. Now the girl's shrieks didn't disturb the denizens of the small island. It was as if they knew she couldn't harm them now. The quicksand had drawn her deeper into its embrace, until just her head and shoulders were out. Slowly, even they had gone from sight. Before that occurred though, Henrietta had stopped struggling. The poison in her system had taken its toll. She had died quietly, finally at rest. The swamp had released her from the madness that had overcome her.

A snake swam across the quicksand, passing over the spot where Henrietta had gone down. The swamp flowers floated in across the quicksand, marking the spot that was to be her grave for eternity.

12

SHERIFF ED LISTENED TO THE thunder and glanced up at the sky. He figured he still had a few hours yet before darkness set in, but the sound of the thunder was something else again. The last thing he wanted was to get trapped back in the swamps if a storm broke out. The storm wasn't that bad by itself, but with a killer stalking them, it would only serve to make things quite a bit worse.

The sheriff walked back and checked on the wounded man. He didn't really care about Zeke Jones one way or the other, but the man was going to cause problems if he didn't hurry up and die. Sheriff Ed examined the wound carefully, stroking the heavy gray beard on his chin as he went over the possibilities he had. Either he could head back toward town, or let the two living brothers take the wounded man back themselves while he and his deputy got onto the bushwacker's trail. There was a problem there too, he reflected. His deputy just might have other plans, since his brother was dead. Jericho might want to bury his brother right away. It was hard to tell what went on in a man's mind, and a man like Jericho was extra hard to figure out.

Sheriff Ed walked over to where Jericho sat beside his dead brother. "Jericho," he began, "I been tryin' to figure out just what we ought to do." He hesitated for a second, to see if the man was listening to what he said. "Now we can take the body back to town and give him a decent funeral while the killer gets away, or we can get on that bastard's trail and run him aground before the sun sets again."

After Ed finished speaking, he stood silently by and waited for the grief-stricken man to make up his mind. There was such an intense, pained look on Jericho's face that Sheriff Ed wondered if the man would be any help after all. Whoever went with him would have to have their mind right, or he'd end up dead.

"I don't reckon it would do no good to take my brother back to town, Ed," Jericho began softly. "He wouldn't have cared about having people at his funeral who didn't bother to speak to him while he was livin', so I reckon I'll find somewhere around here in the back waters and bury him. Maybe I'll make a good marker one day and bring it back, so as I can recognize the spot where he's at."

Jake walked over to the two men. "You ain't got to bury him back here if you don't care too, Jericho. You can take him on up to our place and put him under where my paw's buried at. That is, if you don't mind it, 'cause we'd be right proud havin' him buried on our place."

"I don't reckon I'd mind at all, Jake," Jericho replied. "Fact is, I'd be mighty beholden to you for lettin' me bury him around other white folks."

None of the men missed the insinuation, least of all Jake. When he offered the chance to bury the boy on his property next to his own people, it meant that he was giving the dead man all the respect due another white man. There was no way in the world that he would have offered to bury Jitty on his land if he hadn't been white. It was unheard of in that part of the country to bury a black man next to a white man, no matter how much the black might have been respected.

"That's fine, just fine," Sheriff Ed stated, ready now to get his posse started. "Now we goin' have to fix up somethin' to carry old Zeke on." He was thinking of the time involved. He had received a small break when Jake made his offer. Now he wouldn't have to worry about going all the way back to town first before getting on the trail of the black.

"You got some kind of idea who we might be after, Sheriff?" Jake inquired, as he shifted his rifle around in his arms and stared out over the water to the opposite bank.

"I reckon," Sheriff Ed replied, walking away and speaking over his shoulder, "we better get busy findin' some kind of saplin' that we can make a stretcher out of. With that stomach wound, Zeke goin' be hard to move." Ed walked off into the nearby woods and began searching for a strong sapling, all the time wishing the man would hurry up and pass away. There was nothing they could do for the wounded man. In fact, the sheriff reflected as he ambled through the woods, he didn't believe even a doctor could do anything for Zeke. The man had taken too much buckshot in the stomach. It was just a matter of time now. Sheriff Ed killed as much time as he could back in the woods, praying that Zeke would go ahead and do them the favor of dying. At least they only had to go back to the Jones' farm, and maybe the wounded man wouldn't be too much of a problem. Once they got him there, they could let the women folk fuss over him, and get on about their business.

When the sheriff returned from the woods, Sonny-Boy and Jake had already built a small stretcher. As he approached, they were lifting the unconscious man and placing him on the home-made stretcher.

Zeke cried out in pain, reminding the sheriff that the man was still holding on. Meanwhile, Jericho lifted his dead brother up in his arms and carried him down the bank to their dugout. Sheriff Ed followed, his old shotgun cradled across his arms. He searched the opposite bank, planning on not being taken by surprise again.

After placing Jitty in the bottom of their dug-out, Jericho spoke to the sheriff. "In case somethin' should happen to you, Ed, I think I'm entitled to know who the hell you think it might be we're after." His voice was toneless, revealing none of the emotion his face had betrayed earlier.

Whenever the sheriff was considering something, he was in the habit of stroking his gray beard. Now, as he thought over Jericho's request, his hand went up to his chin. "I reckon you got a point there, Jericho. You never can tell about these things, either. No sir, it just might be my time to go after all."

The sound of thunder cracked overhead. The storm was coming closer. But neither man paid any attention to it. Jericho kept his eyes on the sheriff, waiting for a reply. Sonny-Boy and Jake walked past, carrying their brother. Sheriff Ed waited until they had put him in the dugout.

Jake returned from the river and stood in front of the sheriff.

"I reckon we all would take it kindly if you'd give us your opinion 'bout this ambushin' bastard Ed, 'fore we go off half-cocked and kill up a bunch of niggers," Jake stated harshly, implying that he also had an idea who the ambusher might be.

"Uh-huh," Sheriff Ed began. "Now boys, I want you to know we ain't got no kind of evidence to prove me right, but I got a hunch it's that young black, George." He watched their faces as he spoke, but there was no surprise on them. It was as if both men expected him to say just what he said.

"It's how I figured it, Ed," Jake began. "That nigger been broodin' over what happened to his sister all this time, and just found the balls to try and do something about it."

"It's a little deeper than that," the sheriff answered, watching his deputy closely. "You boys also hung his father, if I remember correctly, so I reckon he had that in mind to when he decided to even up the score."

"Even up the score my ass," Jericho cursed. "My brother ain't done nothin' to him or his family, so he wouldn't have no cause to ambush Jitty like that." There was bewilderment in the man's voice as he spoke, but his eyes were alive. They glittered dangerously as he continued. "No by God, ain't no right in it at all. That nigger done killed Jitty, and somebody goin' pay for it too, you can bet your ass on it!" Jericho turned on his heel and walked quickly toward the waiting boats.

"He got a point there, Sheriff," Jake said as he walked beside the sheriff down to the river. "The boy ain't had no cause to ambush Jitty, so why the hell would he kill a man ain't never done nothin' to him?"

Sheriff Ed didn't know the answer to that one, but he had a good idea. As he thought about it, an alarm went off in his mind. The boy didn't have any reason to kill Jitty, but he had done it. It was possible that the angry black man wanted to kill everyone that was white. Having kept his anger bottled up for so long, anything white would be fair game for the black man. But it went deeper than that. There was something that kept trying to come to the surface in his mind, but Ed just couldn't put his finger on it. There had to be a reason for what George had done. A man didn't just plan something for years, then start killing without some kind of real motivation.

When they reached the dugouts, Sheriff Ed hesitated for a second. Suddenly his old wrinkled face lit up like a Christmas tree. "Boys," he began, "I think I know what's in that coon's mind. Yes sir, I done put my finger right on it. Jake, you and Sonny-Boy take the right side of the river. Me and Jericho, we goin' paddle down the left side. Somewhere between here and you boys' place, that nigger's goin' make his move!"

At the sound of the sheriff's words, Sonny-Boy's face went white as a sheet. "Sheriff, you don't reckon he goin' try and ambush us again, do you?" The fear in the young man's voice was evident. He couldn't conceal the terror that was inside him.

"I reckon he is, Sonny-Boy," Sheriff Ed stated, then asked, "you ain't 'fraid, boy, is you?" The sheriff made a dry sound that was supposed to pass for laughter. "Boy, many times as you went on over to that boy's place and put the meat to his sister, I know you ain't scared now."

Jericho stared coldly at Sonny-Boy. It wasn't hard to read what was in his mind. If it hadn't been for the Jones brothers abusing the girl, his brother would be alive. The only thing that kept his anger from coming down on the Jones brothers was that the killer was still free. Once they had him, Jericho had plans for the brothers who came out of it alive.

"Well I don't give a shit what yo' all think 'bout that nigger," Jake stated. "Me for one ain't 'fraid of him nor anything else black like him. I just pray he gets in the sight of my rifle, that's all."

The sheriff chuckled. "By God, that's right, Jake. That old gun you carry happens to be the one you took from that boy's daddy awhile back, ain't it?"

Jake stared blankly at the sheriff. "I done told you, Sheriff, that nigger sold me this rifle. So when he went and got himself hung, it wasn't 'cause of no old gun!"

The sheriff's laugh was cold and brittle. "I don't have no pity for you Jones boys," he stated, " 'cause you done brought all these problems down on yourselves. I just hate it that I done lost a good deputy because of you bastards!"

It was out in the open now. Without thinking, the sheriff had opened a wound that would have been better all around had it remained closed.

What the brooding Jericho had thought about was now a spoken reality.

"Christ Almighty, Sheriff," Sonny-Boy yelled, "how the hell you figure like that beats the shit out of me!" He glanced out of the corner of his eye to see how Jericho was taking it. What he saw he didn't like. The tall, silent man was glaring at Jake's back. It didn't take a mindreader to know what he was thinking. The man looked like a wild beast of prey, ready to leap on a weaker foe.

Sonofabitch, Sheriff Ed cursed under his breath. Before he even got his posse out of the swamps there would be trouble. He could read the sign, and from what he saw, he didn't like it. He believed that if he didn't watch them closely, he'd have to take Jericho back in handcuffs. Murder was on the man's mind; there was little doubt about it. Now he would have to make sure they stayed apart. If not, Sonny-Boy would end up saying something wrong, and they'd catch pure hell trying to separate the two men. Jake, Sheriff Ed believed, would have enough sense to stay out of the man's way, but Sonny-Boy wouldn't have that kind of sense.

A loud scream of pain came from the Jones' dugout. Damn, if this keeps up, the sheriff thought angrily, the ambusher would hear them coming a mile off. It would make his job a hell of a lot easier knowing that his prey was coming before they even got there.

"Okay now, Jake," Sheriff Ed warned, "you boys keep a sharp watch on your side of the river. Don't forget, whoever the killer is, he plays for keeps!"

The warning was unnecessary. All the men had to do was glance at their dying brother in the bottom of the boat to know that the sniper wasn't playing games.

"Jericho, you better keep your eyes on our side of the river instead of glaring across at them Jones boys," the sheriff warned. "You might not get a chance to put them thoughts of yours to work if you ain't all mighty careful."

Jericho grunted, but he stopped looking across at the two brothers.

The men lowered their dugouts into the water and began poling. The creek became wider, and soon there was fifty feet between the two boats. The small posse made their way down the river in silence, each man now involved personally in the hunt.

Jericho found himself suddenly in the role of an avenger. His thoughts were indeed black. If they ever went ashore and he got the chance, he swore to himself that he'd kill the first Jones brother he could. As his eyes searched the river banks on his side, he fingered the long 30-0-6. The rifle was a new model. Jitty had used the old double-barreled shotgun. It had been decided between the brothers that Jericho would own the new gun while they saved up enough money for a rifle for Jitty.

The thought of Jitty enraged Jericho. He fought down the desire to take his rifle and cut down the two men across from him. He remembered the stories of how the Jones had the child-like black girl trained to come at their whistle. The nights he and Jitty had spent in their small cabin talking about how a man could live with his sister and turn a deaf ear to that whistle coming from the swamps at any time of the night. As Jericho thought about it, he remembered the night he and Jitty had followed the Jones boys from town and watched them from behind some trees as they raped the young girl. He remembered seeing the tall black man who creeped from the rear of his cabin and watched the white men rape his sister over and over again. Many nights after that he and his brother had laid on their separate bunks and talked about it, wondering what went through the black man's mind as he observed his sister being turned into a garbage can for the amusement of the Jones boys.

Lightning flashed across the darkening sky. It was too early for the natural darkness of evening to set in, and the storm was almost upon them.

Jake rode in the front of his dugout, while Sonny-Boy did the poling from the rear. Jake had keener eyesight than his brother, so he took the point. In the sheriff's boat, Jericho rode point. Being a younger man than the sheriff, it was accepted that he had better sight even though the old gray-bearded sheriff was pretty keen-eyed himself.

"Ed," Jericho began, speaking quietly so that his voice wouldn't carry, "you really expect trouble from the boy?"

"Uh-huh. Way I got it figured, Jericho, the boy don't plan on lettin' none of us leave the swamps alive."

"I hadn't thought of it like that," Jericho replied quickly. "I sure in the hell hadn't!" Jericho smiled. If the sheriff was right, then he'd get the chance he was hoping for. Just the opportunity to flush out the killer of his brother, then he could take care of the men who were responsible for the man becoming a killer in the first place.

"Suppose it ain't the boy, Sheriff?" Jericho asked.

"If it ain't the boy, Jericho, I'll eat that shotgun you got."

After a brief silence, Jericho spoke again. "I reckon the boy had reasons for killin' the Jones boys, Ed, but he ain't had no cause to hurt Jitty." Jericho said in a voice cracking with emotion.

"Naw, he ain't had no reason to hurt Jitty, son, so he goin' pay for it. I promise you that much, Jericho, even though it ain't much for the life of your brother. Jitty was a good man, son, as you know. I always respected him, just like I respect you," the sheriff said, then added, "so please don't do nothing that will make me have to hunt you down. These old swamps ain't no fun for an old man like me, and knowing you, you'd do the same thing the coon is doing, hiding out somewhere back in here, causing me to have to spend a lot of time digging you out."

For some reason the normally quiet Jericho wanted to talk. He kept a sharp watch even as he continued to question the sheriff. "I remember that girl Henrietta, Sheriff. She done us a good turn once. I mean, you know how it is, me and my brother ain't never had no book learnin', but that gal took her time and taught Jitty how to write his name. Yes sir, she really done it. He was sure proud of it too!"

The sheriff remained silent, letting the man talk himself out. He knew that the man's moody nature demanded some sort of outlet for the anger that was inside him. He couldn't remain silent, because there was too much to think about.

"Jitty come across her fishin' one day, oh, it was some spell ago. Four, five years ago, Sheriff. Anyhows, she had one of them there books with her, you know, the kind that don't have pictures at all." The man fell silent, trying to get the right words before continuing. "Anyways, Ed, somehow or 'nother, Jitty lets her know he can't read, so right off she begins teachin' him how to read and put his name down on paper. Right after that, she goes off to school somewheres, or Jitty would've learned more then he done from her."

There was nothing the sheriff could think of to say. Jericho continued speaking slowly. "Anyways, Ed, after she come back, and Jitty hears 'bout what happened to her, he takes him a trip back here in the swamps to see for himself. You know, people been talkin' 'bout the change in the girl, so he come and finds out for himself. Well Sheriff, ain't never been nothin' between them but friendship, but after Jitty done seen what them Jones boys done gone and did to that girl, I had one hell of a time keepin' him from stickin' his knife into whichever one he seen."

A vine hanging down gave them a scare. Jericho

used his pole to brush it aside. "Jitty was so shook up by it," Jericho continued after lowering his pole back into the water, "he drug me along one night after the Jones boys did some braggin' in town 'bout where they was going. Well we followed 'em, seen how they used that old gal. Made me mad as hell myself, but I had to hold onto my temper, 'cause Jitty was all for bustin' in on them and killin' the lot. Yes sir, had to damn near drag him away, so I understand why the boy would be wantin' to kill the Jones boys. But for the life of me, can't figure out why he'd ambush Jitty. Just can't figure it out, Ed, just can't see no reason for it unless the boy's gone mad."

"Way I figure it, Jericho, the boy ain't mad at all. He got a plan all right." The sheriff stopped poling for a minute. "The way the boy figures it, Jericho, Jitty had to die." Sheriff Ed waited for his words to reach the man. "Yeah, the nigger got it all planned out. If he gets rid of all of us back here tonight, well, there won't be no witnesses against him, you follow me?"

Jericho shook his head in agreement. "I can see where that makes a little sense," he stated, chewing on the words as if they were a piece of meat.

"You can bet on it," the sheriff continued. "If he knocks us all off back here in the swamps, hell, it ain't enough men in town with balls enough to even come back here searching for the remains. Hell's fire, all they'd do is sit around drinkin' corn likker and wonder whatever happened to the old sheriff and the Jones boys. By the time they got through guessin', Jericho, they'd have you and your brother marked down as the killer, and swear both of you are somewhere back here in the swamps hidin' out!"

Again the silence fell between the men as the sheriff gave Jericho time enough to ponder over his words. When he guessed that Jericho understood what he was saying, he continued. "They'd have to guess that either you and Jitty did it, or possibly the Jones brothers, 'cause they never would give a nigger that much sense or nerve. No sir, it never would enter their minds that a young black man did away with us."

That was something Jericho could understand. He knew the workings of the southern white man's mind. For them to believe that one black man had the nerve to kill five or six white men was beyond comprehension. A black man killing one white man, yes, they could understand that happening. But six white men—impossible—the black man able to do such a thing hadn't been born yet.

"Oh my God, help me Jesus, please oh Lord,"

the cries were loud and clear as Zeke screamed out
in agonizing pain.

Jake started to leave his front seat but the sharp
warning from the sheriff sent him back to his place
in the front of the dugout.

"If you don't keep your eyes peeled, Jake, it
might be more then one wounded man we goin'
end up carrying home," the sheriff called out as he
pointed ahead. "We coming to the big bend, so be
careful, the boy goin' have to make his move soon,
or he'll lose out on his chances.

The big bend was the turn off from the main
body of water. What they were traveling down now
was only a small creek that led into the swamp.
Not all the small creeks led back to the main body
of water, so the trick was not to lose yourself
down one of the many small creeks that led to
nowhere. The creeks wound their way around the
many tiny islands, some of which were completely
covered with water. Getting lost in that maze was
comparable to suicide.

Normally, Jake in the lead boat would have been
a sitting duck. But because he was prepared he gave
himself a chance. As the dugouts approached open
water, the men in both boats began to relax. The
only danger that could come to them now was
from the last island they had passed. As long as

they stayed in the middle of the large lake, there was nothing to fear. They could see everything there was to see, and soon they would be out of the range of any shotgun.

Sheriff Ed didn't think George could have a good rifle in his possession. The only weapons the boy had to his knowledge was the old shotgun, and maybe a hunting knife. The last island they had passed was the ambusher's only possibility until they neared the creeks that led to the farms of the Jones family.

Just as the men relaxed and exchanged their poles for the oars, the shotgun blast came from the island they had just passed. As soon as the wily sheriff heard the first shot, he dropped down into the bottom of the dugout beside the body of Jitty. The second shot came right on the heels of the first one. The sheriff could hear the buckshot hitting the sides of the dugout and he thanked the Lord for not making it possible for the bushwacker to have a rifle. If he had had a long-range rifle, the men in the slow moving boats would have been gone.

As the sheriff kept his head down, he heard the shots coming from the front of his boat. Jericho was returning the fire of the bushwacker, taking his time and firing with a slow cadence.

The sounds of repeated firing came from the other boat as Jake emptied his rifle into the shadows of the island they had just passed. He fired without aiming, content to fire off as many rounds as he could. It is always that way when a desperate man shoots for his life. Sonny-Boy had been hit by the first blast and knocked from the boat, Jake had watched his brother go into the water then had turned and begun shooting with reckless abandon towards the source of the shotgun blasts.

13

GEORGE WATCHED THE SKY CLOSELY, hoping that the coming storm would reach him before the men came out of the swamps. It would be a help, he reasoned, if the rain would come down. In the darkness of the storm, he would be able to move closer to his prey without being seen.

His eyes searched the small islands as he poled slowly down the creek. It would have to be just the right spot if he wanted to come out of it alive. He was sure he could get one of the men, but he knew that as soon as he fired at them they would return his fire using better rifles.

The long-range rifles that some of the posse carried made it mandatory that he pick the perfect spot for his ambush. He didn't want to just kill one of them and let the rest escape. As he searched the nearby river banks, he promised himself that he'd make sure this time to kill at least one of the Jones boys. He reflected bitterly on the killing of the deputy. He remembered the man and regretted having shot him, but it had been necessary. The deputy had been one of the few white men who had been kind toward them. He remembered the man from his last visit to their cabin. He had shown up one morning and asked to see Henrietta. When he had told him that Henrietta wasn't there, the tall dark-complexioned man had pushed past him and gone into the cabin where Henrietta had been sitting. After a few minutes the man returned, and George could have sworn there were tears in the man's eyes as he walked away from George, swearing under his breath.

After that George had seen the man only one more time. He had come from down river, traveling over the land. In his hands he carried a small bag. This time he didn't ask for Henrietta, he just held out the bag for George. As soon as George had taken it, the man had turned around and left. George figured it must have been at least a fifteen mile walk coming the way the man had come. After he left, George opened the bag and saw that it contained jawbreakers, the candy that Henrietta loved to eat.

Yes, he reflected, it had been a very bitter thing he had done. Had he taken his time and noticed which white man he was sighting down on, he would have held his fire, but he hadn't seen him until after the man had fallen. Then it was much too late. Now, he knew the man's brother would never give up until he killed George, or George killed him. George had never known their names, but he knew them on sight. Two quiet white men who minded their own business and they were both good hunters. George was sure of that after spying on them a couple of times when he saw them back in the swamps.

Finally George came to the last island before reaching the large lake that led to the Jones' farm. If he didn't do it here, he'd have to row down to the farm and wait for them there. He quickly rejected the idea of ambushing them at the farm. It was much too dangerous an idea. Even if he were lucky enough to bring down one or two of the men, the others could easily overtake him in the open water as he rowed back into the swamps.

No, he'd have to make his ambush work from

here, the last island. The one thing that was in his favor, was that by the time they reached here, they would begin to relax. After sweating their way past all the narrow islands, they would almost certainly begin to feel as if they were home free.

Having made up his mind to ambush them from the last island before the big bend, George debated with himself on whether or not he'd have enough time to take his dugout around the island and place it where it would do the best good. If he could hide it on the other side of the island, he'd have it made. Once he cut loose on the white men, all he'd have to do would be to make a run for his boat. If the white men pursued him, he'd just have to reach his boat before they caught him and shove off. Then the white men would be left on the island without their boats. They'd have to retrace their steps all the way back to where they had landed before they could continue the chase.

By that time, George figured he could cut back into his well concealed waterway and head for home. What was left of the posse would never find out which waterway he took away from the open lake. It was a good plan except for the fact it meant that some of the posse would be left alive. He desperately wanted to kill them all. Maybe, thought George, he could stay on the island and kill them one at a time as they tried to track him down. It was possible, if he moved right, but it would be touch and go. Each man he was after was a well-armed hunter. Each one had had experience in hunting down black men, so he would be up against well-trained men. Whatever the odds, he had to make sure he did a good, complete job. If he left one man alive it would mean that Henrietta would have to live the rest of her life in the back swamps, because he would never be able to come out. As George thought about it, he realized that the sheriff would never give up hunting him, until one of them was dead. So be it, he reasoned, it was to be to the death. As long as he was able to drop all of the Jones boys, he would be able to die in peace.

George thought about Henrietta, and hoped that she stayed in the cabin until he returned. If she left it, she might get lost trying to find her way among the weed-covered trails. Then there was always the threat of the quicksand. George cursed himself for not taking the time to show her the quicksand, so she would have known about it. But as he thought about it, he realized that it wouldn't have done any good, because ten minutes after he explained it to her, she would have forgotten what he had told her.

No, the swamps were no place for Henrietta. She couldn't last a month unless he stayed right beside her. He wondered if it might be possible to take her along with him whenever he had to hunt. It would be the only way, he was sure of it. He promised himself that once he got back, he'd never leave her alone again. No matter what he had to do, he'd just have to drag her along.

If that was the case, George reasoned, the only recourse he had was to play the game out to the end right here and now. He picked up his oars and rowed around the bend. He moved swiftly now. He wanted to find a place to hide the boat, not so much for an escape, but somewhere where the whites couldn't find it once they came ashore. Whether they knew it or not, the island would be their battle ground. George was determined not to leave until every last white was dead.

George patted the shotgun shells he had in his pocket. Only ten were left. If he could cut down the old sheriff and somehow reach the body, he could get his hands on some more shells. It was something to keep in mind, he reflected. Also, there was the chance of knocking off Jake Jones, then he could get his hands on his father's rifle. If he succeeded in doing that, he would be keeping the promise he made over his father's grave—to one day kill the bastard that had killed him for the rifle. Just the thought of it filled George with a stormy rage. Jake Jones had been a curse to his family ever since he could remember. But if things went right this day, he'd more than even the score. There wouldn't be a Jones brother left alive.

An old oak tree that had been struck by lightning sometime in the past caught his attention. He rowed the dugout toward it, wary of any snakes that might have made the old limbs their home. Some of the roots were buried deep in the water and he moved around them carefully. This would be one hell of a time to get a snake bite. It would be the end of the white men's worry, because this far away from any medical help, he'd be lost. The blood poisoning would set in before he could even reach his cabin in the swamps.

The bank was high. George had to struggle with the boat to get it up out of the water. Once on dry land, he pulled and pushed until he got the dugout completely out of the water, but he couldn't find anywhere close at hand to conceal it. If for any reason, he had to leave in a hurry, he'd have a hell of a time getting it back into the water. But that was the chance he'd have to take. He glanced out over the water. There was the bend on the left that led back toward his cabin and it wouldn't take but a few minutes of fast rowing before he reached it. Still, his back would be exposed to the men with rifles as he rowed toward the turn off. Once again, he was convinced that he would have to kill everybody on the island before he attempted to make his run.

George got behind the dugout and shoved it deeper into the wooded section. He stopped and wiped his brow. All he needed now was to cover the boat up real good with brush and a few weeds, so that the men who would be searching for him wouldn't find it. It would be a fatal irony if they tried to escape the death trap he had planned for them with his very own boat—an irony he knew would plague him forever.

Once he finished covering the boat, George stood back and examined his work carefully. Noticing a slight gap in the camouflage, he searched the nearby terrain until he found some tall weeds. With the help of his long hunting knife he quickly cut them loose and carried the weeds back to the dugout to stick them over the gap. Again he stepped back and checked on his work. It wouldn't fool anyone who was searching for the boat, he thought, but it would pass as scenery to anybody who didn't know where to look.

Satisfied with his work, George picked up his

shotgun and started across the small island. He searched the brush ahead of him. Even with the heavy, high-backed boots he wore, he was taking a chance with the snakes. He started to search for a green branch. As soon as he saw one about the size he needed he stopped and cut it down. After that, George could breathe a lot easier. The brush was too dense for a man to try and travel through without some kind of stick. He used the pole as he walked, striking the ground ahead of him to arouse any of the poisonous reptiles that might be in his path.

Before he had finished crossing the island the stick paid off. Right before he went through some heavy brush, he stuck the stick down into the high weeds and swung it back and forth. A loud hissing sound came to him. He backed up quickly, searching the nearby ground.

As if drawn from its lair, a long dark-colored snake came wiggling out. The reptile was in an ill mood, angry because something had the nerve to disturb it. As George watched it work toward him slowly, his mouth formed the unspoken words. Cottonmouth, the most vicious snake in the swamps. Ill-tempered most of the time, ready to bite at all times. As the snake began to coil, George could see the white spot inside the open mouth that gave it its name.

Without hesitation he stepped forward and brought the stick down across the snake's curling body. Better for him to launch the attack than to wait for the snake to decide to strike. The stick was too thin to really kill the long, heavy-bodied snake, but it did what George hoped for. As the snake came out of its coil, George struck it again across the back. This time the long branch broke in half. Using the short half that he was left with, George swung it like a baseball bat. His constant attack on the reptile kept the snake from curling up into its deadly coil. The unrelenting attack made the fully aroused snake change its mind. Instead of wanting to attack his assailant, now the reptile only wanted to escape. Water was its domain and as soon as the chance presented itself the snake gave up the brief skirmish and slithered into the thick underbrush toward a less demanding environment.

George shook his head and wiped the sweat from his brow. It could have been a hell of a lot worse, he reasoned, as he thanked his lucky stars for taking the time to pick up the stick. Now that the danger was past, he didn't let his guard down. Pit vipers were everywhere, this being the time of the year for the young ones to come forth. Once a water moccasin gave birth to its young ones, they were on their own. They didn't come from an egg. Like humans, the baby water moccasins were born live.

Once again the sound of thunder shattered the stillness of the swamps and the birds and other small animals went wild, frightened by the roar. The birds flew from one tree to another, then back where they had started from. In the underbrush the larger animals moved about nervously. Threats of rain in the swamps could spell danger for many of the inhabitants. Water would seep down into their lair and drown many of them, while others would be trapped in the sand pits and other small holes used for shelter.

The pathways became less dense as George neared the river bank. He caught himself breathing hard from the earlier exertion. Unknowingly he had picked up the pace as he neared the river and was almost running. He had to be careful because the woods carried sounds over extreme distances.

When George heard the voices from the river, he began to run, disregarding the dangers underfoot. When he reached the river bank he saw that he was almost too late. He cursed silently. In another minute he would have missed his victims. As he peered out of the brush he could see instantly that he would never be able to ambush as many of the posse as he had hoped to.

Without hesitating, George raised the shotgun to his shoulder and took aim; if he wasted another second, the men in the dugouts would be out of the range of his shattergun. As he took aim, he cursed inwardly as he recognized the man in his sights. Instead of it being the hated Jake Jones, it was the cowardly Sonny-Boy. Well, he reassured himself, since he meant to kill all of them eventually, he'd have to be satisfied with just Sonny-Boy for now. Because of the way the men had placed the dugouts, it would be impossible for him to knock off more than just one.

The recoil of the shotgun slammed him backward. Before he could really take good aim, he raised the weapon and fired again. Quickly he broke the gun down and inserted two more shells. By the time he got the gun back into firing position, rifle bullets began to thump loudly against the trees, and whistle overhead.

George took the shotgun down from his shoulder as he watched the frantic efforts of the men out on the water. Since they were now out of his range, he could only observe their actions. He smiled coldly as he watched Sonny-Boy keel over and fall into the water.

Finally, Jake stopped firing his rifle and went to the aid of his brother. George started to raise the shotgun to his shoulder, but realized that it would be a wasted effort. The men were definitely out of range now. The underwater current had slowly moved the awkward dugouts down river.

George watched as Jake, struggling to get his brother back in the boat, fell overboard. The oldest brother grabbed the lifeless body and clung to it, sobbing like a baby. Jake knew instantly that Sonny-Boy was dead. He cursed in frustration, but every time he opened his mouth he took in water.

Using as much caution as possible, Sheriff Ed worked his boat over until he was beside the empty dugout. With Jericho and the sheriff, Jake finally got Sonny-Boy and himself back into the boat. Then, with Jericho scaning the river bank for any sign of the sniper, they slowly rowed the two boats back towards the island, making sure to give a lot of room to the area from which they suspected the shotgun shots had come.

George watched them approach, seeing that they hoped to land down river from where he was. He moved back into the brush and started making his way towards the approaching men.

"That sonofabitch is going to be waitin' for us, Jericho," the sheriff stated, his eyes probing the bushes and trees surrounding the island's river bank.

"I hope the bushwackin' cocksucker don't get away," Jake yelled from his boat. He glared down at his two brothers stretched out on the bottom of the boat.

"Just have a little patience, Jake," the sheriff cautioned. "Our boy is waitin', you can bet on it." He hesitated, then continued. "Jericho, if that nigger was watchin', he's runnin' like hell right now through the brush tryin' to cut us off, so I'd think the best bet for us would be to swing way around the island and come back on foot."

"I reckon," Jericho answered abruptly. All he wanted was to get a clean shot at whoever was ambushing them.

Jake cursed fruitlessly. The men were tired and angry, fear was riding on their shoulders. Each man felt it in a certain way. While the sheriff desired to meet it head on, he still felt a fear like he had never known before.

"Swing wider, Jericho," the sheriff instructed. "We don't want to give that bastard another shot at us."

Jericho mumbled something under his breath, but he still followed the sheriff's instructions. "I don't reckon that coon can run through them bushes as fast as we can move down the river," Jericho stated, keeping his eyes turned toward the danger area.

"That's sure in the hell right," Ed answered. "I reckon we ain't got to go much farther 'for we goin' put our feet on some dry land."

No matter how hard Jake rowed, he couldn't keep up with the sheriff. When he glanced up and saw Sheriff Ed turning toward the shore, he felt relief. There were few men, he believed, who could move through some woods as silently as he could. If the nigger hadn't left, he was sure they could flush him out. And what a time he'd have then, he thought coldly. If he had anything to do with it, he swore silently that he would personally cut the black bastard's nuts off.

All three of the men breathed easier once they reached the river's bank without being shot at. Being out on the river made them feel like sitting ducks. Quickly the three men pulled the two boats out of the water, then removed Sonny-Boy from the bottom of the dugout and placed him on dry land.

A blind rage overcame Jake as he examined the wound in his brother's back. "The dirty sonofa-bitch shot Sonny-Boy in the back," he swore angrily, then grabbed the sheriff's arm and made him look at the wound. "You see that, Ed, done shot my brother in the back, the cowardly black bastard!" Jake broke down sobbing loudly and holding his head in his hands, as he went to his knees.

The sheriff looked away. "Jake, you better pull yourself together, old boy. You got another brother here who needs your help."

At the mention of his name, Zeke let out a groan. The pain in his stomach had stopped for a minute. When he twisted around, all he could see were the sides of the dugout. He tried to cry out for the men to come and get him out of the boat, but no words came from his lips.

"I reckon we better set out, Ed," Jericho stated looking warily around the heavily weeded area. "Somebody goin' have to stay here with Zeke, Sheriff. I don't reckon he'd like wakin' up and findin' everybody gone."

Sheriff Ed began to rub his jaw. "Jake, I reckon the job falls to you to see that your brother is all right. We can't just go stalkin' off into the woods and leave him alone."

Jake looked up angrily from where he knelt in the dirt. "By God, Ed, you can't do it. I got just as much right to go after that coon as the next man!" He turned to Jericho and glared, his jaw sticking

200

out like a bulldog's.

"It ain't that we want to leave you behind, Jake," the sheriff began, "but it's your brother, and some damn body should stay and look after him. Hell's fire, you can't tell what might happen if we go off and leave him here by himself."

"We just wasting time standin' 'round fussin' 'bout it, Ed," Jericho stated. "If we hurry, we might just catch us a coon runnin' crazy through the woods." As he talked he fingered his late model rifle. All he wanted was one good shot at the coon, then he'd see about takin' care of the remaining Jones boys.

Lightning broke out over them, followed by the sound of thunder. The sky darkened as the men stood there arguing and they realized at once that the rain had finally caught up with them. Large drops began to fall with increasing regularity.

"I reckon we done said everything we can, Jake, so we best be gettin' on if we hope to catch that boy before he runs for cover." The sheriff knew the man they sought wouldn't be hunting for cover. Somewhere out there in the woods a crazy black man was hunting for them, just as they would be hunting for him. Nothing would stop the man, the sheriff knew, but death.

"How you reckon we oughta go 'bout doing

this, Sheriff?" Jericho inquired. "I mean, should we split up so we can cover more ground, or work together?"

"We'll stay together for a while, Jericho. This boy is dangerous as all hell!"

Jericho shrugged his shoulders and started down the river bank. Neither man glanced back at Jake as they left. After they had gone a few feet, the sheriff spoke up.

"I don't reckon we ought to stick by the river bank," he said as he stopped and broke off a long slim green branch. Sheriff Ed tossed the stick to Jericho, then broke off another one for himself. "We best not be takin' too many chances, boy. Walkin' down near the edge of the river ain't doing nothin' but invitin' trouble."

"I reckon you right 'bout that," Jericho answered as he waved his stick back and forth, weighing its balance. "It's more pit vipers crawling around down near the water than it is back in the brush."

The sheriff agreed with him. "Seems to me we might do better if we headed in a little more deeper, Jericho, but I think our coon is huggin' the river banks searching for us, since he don't know where we pulled in."

Suddenly, Sheriff Ed saw some motion out of

the corner of his eye. He stopped abruptly in his tracks. Jericho came up beside him. "It ain't nothin' but a blue racer," Jericho said, as they watched the fast moving snake disappear into the nearby brush.

"Well, let's hope the rest of them crawling bastards we come across turn out to be racers too," the sheriff stated. There was a note of relief in his voice. Blue racers would leave a man alone if the man left them alone. Being too swift to catch, the gracefully moving reptiles wanted only their isolation.

Jericho let out a laugh. "I reckon you thinkin' along the same lines as me, Ed. Praying we don't stumble over some of them onery ass cottonmouths. If we should happen to," he continued, "these little switches you plucked up ain't goin' be much use."

Sheriff Ed patted his pistol. "I reckon I got somethin' here that will handle any cottonmouth we might come across."

"Yeah," Jericho drawled slowly, "I reckon it will put any of 'em out of their troubles. Only problem 'bout that bucket of grapes is that we need to see them black bastards before we feel one of 'em."

It was impossible for the sheriff not to understand what his deputy was getting at. The sky had darkened and now the swamp was getting pitch black. Soon neither man would be able to see his hand in front of him. If they stumbled over any snakes there would be no warning, only the sudden pain where the reptile had struck. As the sheriff thought about it, he reached back on his belt and removed his flashlight.

"It's goin' be blacker than a witches heart in a few more minutes, Jericho, so if you want to go back to the dugouts, I can well understand it."

"You ought to know better than that, Ed. That coon done killed my kid brother. Ain't no way I'd turn back now, though I hate being caught in any swamp at night. I'll go on until I see that nigger stretched out in front of us!" Jericho removed his flashlight and switched it on. "I reckon if that black boy can run around out here huntin' for us, we can do the same thing to that black sonofabitch."

"I reckon you got a point there," the sheriff answered, leading the way away from the river bank. As he moved deeper into the swamps, he realized it wasn't only the black man he feared. He also feared the unknown, the sudden death that lay in wait for anybody foolhearted enough to walk through the back waters when darkness fell.

14

WHEN THE STORM BROKE, it broke suddenly. Rain came down in a heavy downpour. George stayed close to the river bank, wondering how far down the sheriff and his remaining posse had gone.

The rain was a blessing in one way, and a curse in another. Most of the water snakes would be coming out of their dens and moving to the river. As darkness settled over the swamp, George cursed himself silently for leaving the flashlight. Now he was at the mercy of the elements.

After passing the third large snake that he couldn't identify, he started working his way away from the river. It was too dangerous to be close to

the water, he reasoned, as he went into the brush.
The rain felt good on his skin. For a minute he
debated on whether or not he should take off his
shirt. The rain water would feel good on his bare
skin, but later it would turn cold. He felt his
stomach grumbling and realized that he hadn't
eaten all day.

It would soon be over, he told himself as he
cautiously went through the dense brush. A hanging vine gave him a sudden start. He pushed it back
from his path and continued on. After swinging the
new green branch, broken down to replace the
broken one he had used on the reptile earlier, he
would take a couple of steps. It was slow progress,
but it was the only way he could be sure he didn't
step on some pit viper. The long pole that he used
disturbed the creatures that were in his path. He
only had to swing it and then wait, straining his
eyes to make sure that whatever he disturbed went
on its angry way.

Once, George pulled back the pole and found
that a large snake had wrapped itself around the
end of it. Frantically, he smashed the pole against
the nearest tree, shaking the reptile loose.

Suddenly, to his right, George saw a light flashing through the trees. He knew at once what it was.
He hid behind a wide oak tree and waited until the

by Donald Goines

men were opposite him. He could barely dis-
tinguish the outline of the two figures. Once, when
the man in the rear moved his flashlight, George
saw the sheriff clearly. He wanted to move closer,
so that he could get a better shot if Jake Jones
happened to be the man in the rear. The sounds of
their voice came to him and he suddenly understood what had happened. One of the men had
stayed back at the boat, and if that was the case, it
meant that Zeke must still be alive. George closed
his eyes and tried to remember everything he had
seen when he had first ambushed them.

He remembered how much care the men had
taken with Zeke. Could the hillbilly still be alive?
He had taken a full load of buckshot right in the
gut. If Zeke was indeed still alive, it would explain
why Jake wasn't along with the sheriff. George
couldn't think of any other reason for the man not
being out in the woods searching for him. He was
sure it wasn't from fear. After seeing two of his
brothers cut down, Jake would be roaring to get on
his trail.

The men passed in easy reach of George's shotgun range, but he decided to let them pass. He
could always circle around and cut them off whenever they decided to give up the senseless chase in
the darkness. It wouldn't take them much longer

207

to realize just how stupid it was for them to be stumbling around in the brush.

Before the sound of the men's voices had grown dim, George had started to make his way toward where they had come from. He realized at once that he would have to get back to the river bank and follow it, if he had any hope of ever finding Jake. Without hesitating, he started in the direction of the river. Now, he moved fast, taking the risks he hadn't taken before. His prey was somewhere ahead of him and he meant to find it. It couldn't have happened any better if he had planned it himself.

George was hardly ten minutes down the trail when the sheriff tossed up his hand. "Jericho, I been a fool many times in the past, and might be one many times in the future, but boy, we are doing one of the most damn foolish stunts a man ever did!"

Even before the sheriff said it, Jericho knew what he was going to say. It was foolish of them to be out in the swamps searching for a man in the pitch blackness that surrounded them. At first, before it got dark, it had seemed like a good idea. But now, when they really had a chance to experience the darkness, the truth came home. If the black man was crazy enough to be trying to find his way around in the darkness, all they had to do was sit back at the dugouts and let the swamp do their work for them.

"Gawd dang," the sheriff roared and stopped abruptly.

Jericho, following close behind, almost bumped into him. "What the hell!" he yelled, almost dropping his rifle.

"Take you a good look at what we almost stumbled into," Sheriff Ed stated, then flashed his light in front of them.

At the sight of the quicksand in front of them, Jericho let out a sigh. "Well old timer, looks like the boy won this round after all."

"Just for a day," Ed replied sharply. "As soon as the sun comes up we'll be out lookin' for him. I don't reckon he'll go too far, seein' as he got the same idea as we have," the sheriff stated, nodding his shaggy head in agreement with his own words. "Yeah, that boy wants a crack at us just as bad as we want one at him. Hell's fire, Jericho, he ain't going nowhere at all!"

Even though both men had admitted their failure, they were both reluctant to turn around and go back. "Ain't no reason for us to fool ourselves, Jericho. Whenever old swamp hounds like us damn near walk smack into some quicksand, it's time to stop and take stock of just what the hell we're doing."

Without answering, Jericho wheeled around and started back the way they had come. For some reason he had a guilty feeling. It was as if he was quiting on Jitty. Jitty wouldn't have given up the trail of the man who bushwacked his brother, that was one thing Jericho was sure of. But this fumbling around in the dark wasn't getting them anywhere either. They could come within five feet of the nigger, Jericho reasoned, and they'd never know he was there. After all, the man was dark-skinned, so they wouldn't stand a chance of seeing him in this blackness.

After getting on the sheriff's back trail, George moved down the hidden path swiftly. When he reached the river he slowed down slightly but continued on. He would have passed by the small camp in the darkness if he hadn't heard Zeke cry out in pain.

At the sound of the wounded man's voice, George swung around and followed his nose. He could smell smoke. As he approached, he saw Jake bending down over a tiny fire that was about to go out because of the rain.

"Jake, Jake," his ailing brother called. "Boy, you got to do somethin' for me. The pain, boy, I can't stand the pain. It feels like somebody done poured boiling oil down inside me!"

Once George knew where the men were, he removed the pistol from under his belt. Before the two brothers knew what was happening, George was standing in the small clearing they were using for their camp. Jake had his back to George, kneeling down over his only surviving brother. Never in his life had Jake shown so much kindness to Zeke. It had dawned on him that Zeke was the only brother he had left alive. The very thought of it filled him with a killing rage toward the black man who had done this to his family. If he could only see the nigger, he thought coldly, he would kill the jig with his bare hands!

"Now that's what I call a right pretty sight," George stated quietly as he walked up behind Jake.

The tall white man jumped as though someone had stuck him with a knife. "By gawd," he roared, "you got the nerve . . ." His eyes went to the pistol George held, causing him to stop. "That's Jamie's pistol, boy. You done really did somethin' to my young brother."

George laughed in his face. "Naw, I ain't did nothing to him. Them 'gators back in the pond did it for me. Yes sir, them 'gators had a damn good time on all that stinkin' white meat!"

As he spoke, Jake's eyes grew large and cold. "Boy, tell me the truth. You just funnin' me, ain't you? We ain't did you no harm that would make you put my brother in that 'gator pool." He didn't want to believe it, even though he knew what the tall black man said was the truth.

"Jake," Zeke managed to say, " that ain't the nigger who hurt me, is it? Jake. . . ." Both of the men ignored the sick man's words as they locked wills with each other.

"You hear that?" George inquired. "I'm sure glad that white bastard didn't die right off when I put them shotgun shells in his stomach. I couldn't have hoped for anything better." George laughed, wildly, as he looked from one brother to the other.

Jake finally realized that the young black meant to kill him. It was like an awakening. "Boy, now you just listen to me. The sheriff goin' be back in a second, so you just give me that pistol, you hear?"

George laughed again, this time it was even wilder. "I sure plan on givin' it to you, honkie," he said, calmly pulling the trigger. The bullet caught Jake in the stomach, spinning him around. As he fell to his knees, George approached and grabbed the front of the man's shirt. Raising the pistol, he brought it down sharply and broke the man's nose. The force of the blow tore Jake loose from the hold George had on his shirt.

"My gawd, boy," Zeke managed to say. "You done went and shot old Jake." His voice wavered with disbelief and pain. As Jake fought back the pain that rushed up from his stomach, he could feel the boy pulling at his pants. He opened his eyes and blinked up at the black man.

"Boy, what you goin' do?" Jake whined, sounding like a beggar. "Please, boy, don't hurt old Jake. I ain't never done you no dirt," he cried, as he felt the dirty long johns ripped away from his body. Even with the cold rain falling on him, he could feel the black man's cold hands on his privates. His penis shriveled up, as though it knew what was about to happen. "Please, boy, please," Jake screamed, watching in horror as the tall black man removed his hunting knife from his belt.

Without wasting any motions, George got a good grip on the tiny white penis and started to cut. The man's screams were music to his ears.

"Nigger, nigger, what you doing to my brother?" Zeke cried out over the screams of his brother. He tried to raise himself up but fell back. What little strength he had was being drained by fear.

George stopped for a second. "Why, I ain't doing nothing more than I'm going to do for you,

Zeke. You just wait your turn." George returned to his butcher's work and, before he had finished, Jake had passed out from the pain.

George bent down and shoved the tiny white piece of meat into Jake's mouth. The way the man was bleeding, George didn't believe he could live. To make sure, he leaned over and cut the small, dirty bag that held the man's nuts. When he raised back up, he glanced around to see where he could put them.

"These is the most useless things I ever saw," George remarked casually as he approached Zeke. Without a backward glance, he tossed the sac back toward the tiny fire.

Zeke stared at the man as he approached. The sight of what had happened to Jake had completely taken his mind off his stomach wound. He attempted to get up and run, but he was wounded too badly.

"George," Zeke begged, using the black man's first name for the first time in his life. "George, I'm hurt already, boy. You done gut shot me, so ain't that enough?"

George didn't waste any time. He used the knife to cut away the man's pants. Quickly he bent over and repeated the butchering job he had done on Jake. Zeke's screams were not as loud as his

by Donald Goines

brother's and before George had finished cutting on the man, he died.

The two men had just reached the river's edge when they heard the pistol shot. Jericho glanced back at the sheriff. "You reckon it's what I think it is?"

Sheriff Ed shook his shoulders. He couldn't be sure. It wasn't thunder or lightning though. That he was sure of. "You just be careful, Jericho. I'd hate for somethin' to happen to you at this here stage of the game."

The men moved swiftly now and the sound of a bull alligator came to them. Jericho took his eyes off the trail for a second and glanced back at the sheriff.

"You know as well as I do, Jericho, that ain't what we heard," Ed stated, as he brought up the rear. "You just better keep that darn light of yours on what's ahead of you."

The sound of a scream came to them. It didn't sound human at first, but when it was repeated, both men knew it was a man. The scream was terrible, a cry of pure horror and pain that came from deep within the victim's soul. The sheriff tried to move faster.

Jericho took his eyes off the ground and glanced back at the sheriff.

"Goddamn, Ed," Jericho exclaimed. Then his feet slipped in the muddy bank and Jericho began to fall.

Instantly, the sheriff flashed his light down the bank as Jericho rolled. The beam fell on a dark shape coming out of the water. The sheriff yelled out a warning.

"Watch it, Jericho. On your left, boy, it's a viper."

Jericho couldn't break his fall, but he could throw his body to the right, changing his direction. As he slipped down the muddy bank, Sheriff Ed grabbed at his holstered pistol.

The sudden arrival of the man sliding down the bank disturbed the huge water snake. It began to go into a coil at once. Jericho was too much of an expert to be bitten without putting up a defense. He had been fond of saying that any man who saw a snake and still was bitten by it was a fool.

As the reptile went into its coil, Jericho brought his rifle over. Laying in the mud of the bank he half sat up as he swung the rifle like a baseball bat, catching the snake with a solid blow. The sound of the barrel hitting the reptile was loud. He lifted the snake up from the bank and knocked it back into the darkened water.

"He didn't hit you, did he boy?" the sheriff

asked sharply as he kept the flashlight moving around the muddy bank, trying to see if there were any more vipers about.

Jericho shook his head as he got up and made his way back up the small incline. "Naw, he didn't hit me, Ed, but he scared the shit out of me! If you hadn't swung your light down there when you did, I'd never have seen the bastard," Jericho said, wiping the mud from his pants. "I reckon my flashlight fell into the river," he finished lamely.

"Don't worry about it," Ed stated, then fell silent as loud screams came from the camp the two men had left. "You better check on your rifle, though!"

Ed led the way back toward camp, moving fast. They came up on the camp from the river bank, each man walking softly. The sight they saw shook both men deeply. As they watched, Zeke was screaming for the last time.

The sheriff stepped out into the clearing. "Okay boy," he began, but that was as far as he got. The tall black youth moved with the swiftness of a panther. His back had been turned to the men, and at the sound of the sheriff's voice, George dropped to one knee and came up with the long-barreled pistol. The sheriff was taken completely by surprise. The young black had moved so fast, that the shotgun was almost useless to the old man. Even as the sheriff pulled the trigger, he realized he had fired over the kneeling man's head.

Before George could pull the trigger of his pistol, Jericho stepped around the sheriff and shot him in the chest. The high-powered rifle made a thumping sound as the long shell struck the boy, knocking him off his feet.

Pain exploded in George's chest and he suddenly remembered Henrietta. He had to get up and get back to her. He managed to fight his way back to his knees, but Jericho fired again. This time the force of the blow took him backwards and down the river bank. The black waters of the river surrounded him and welcomed him. The black waters of the swamp had finally gotten their man.

THE END

INNER CITY HOODLUM

BY DONALD GOINES

Smack, numbers, money and murder trap a struggling youngblood! Johnny Washington, a teenage Black in Los Angeles, knows the freight yards like the back of his hand. He and his pals Josh and Buddy hit them often, ripping off the boxed up treasures for a fence. They have to. They're the sole support of their families. But when Josh is killed by a trigger-happy security guard and Buddy scatters his brains with nunchaku sticks, they leave the yards for others to try to etch a place in the jungle. Elliot Davis, better known as the Duke, comes to their aid, offering them a place in his ghetto numbers kingdom. But when the Duke recruits Johnny's sister for his stable and later OD's her, Johnny and Buddy come on with a vengeance!

WHITE MAN'S JUSTICE, BLACK MAN'S GRIEF

BY DONALD GOINES

Goines' classic novel of prison life, it has been called "one of the most revealing books ever written about prison life and bigotry built into our system." This is the story of Chester Himes, who thought he was the baddest man to come down the street. Behind prison walls he was nothing more than fresh meat.

DONALD GOINES, savagely gunned down at the age of 39, was the undisputed master of the Black Experience novel. He lived by the code of the streets and exposed in each of his 16 books the rage, frustration and torment spinning through the inner city maze. Each of his stories, classics in the Black Experience genre, were drawn from reality.

CRIME PARTNERS

BY DONALD GOINES

In this powerful novel Donald
Goines lays bare the bloody,
brutal world of crime in the
black ghetto. *Crime Partners* is
a gutsy, sometimes shocking
story of Billy and Jackie, ex-
prison buddies hot on the trigger to pull any job that pays the
bread; of Benson, a black detective and his white partner
Ryan, companions in the right
against black organized crime;
and of Kenyatta, a ghetto chieftain torn between two ambi-
tions: cleaning the ghetto of all
the drug traffic and gunning
down all the white cops! This is
a book that will grip you from
first page to last!

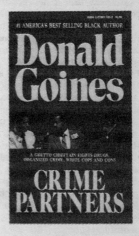

DOPEFIEND

THE STORY OF A BLACK JUNKIE

BY DONALD GOINES

Donald Goines is a talented writer who learned his craft and sharpened his skills in the ghetto slums and federal penitentiaries of America. **DOPEFIEND** is the shocking first novel by the young man who would go on to write sixteen books; books that made him a household name among readers of black literature.

DOPEFIEND exposes the dark, despair-ridden, secret world few outsiders know about—the private hell of the black heroin addict. Trapped in the festering sore of a major American ghetto, a young man and a girl—both handsome, talented, full of promise—are inexorably pulled into the living death of the hardcore junkie.

DOPEFIEND is an appalling story because it rings so true. It is also a work of rare power and great compassion. **DOPEFIEND** will draw you into a nightmare world you will not soon forget.

KENYATTA'S LAST HIT

BY DONALD GOINES

Ghetto chieftain Kenyatta, the living black legend, concentrates his army's ruthless forces to rid the black community of rampant drug traffic. With the help of Elliot Stone, a black football star and latest recruit to the army, Kenyatta discovers the identity of the number one man...the fat cat king of the drug pushers!

The crack black and white detective team, Benson and Ryan, follow Kenyatta's trail of blood across the country. They're not sure now whether their target is the hated butcher they've believed him to be, or the savior of the black community.

But Kenyatta doesn't give a damn. He has only one goal; the fight to the death with the smack king.

This book is the last in the great Kenyatta adventure series written by the late Donald Goines under the Al C. Clark pseudonym.

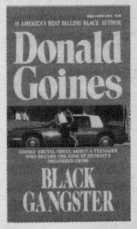